Hi, I'm JIMMY!

Like me, you probably noticed the world is run by adults.

But ask yourself: Who would do the best job

of making books that *kids* will love?

Yeah. **Kids!**

So that's how the idea of JIMMY books came to life.

We want every JIMMY book to be so good

that when you're finished, you'll say,

"PLEASE GIVE ME ANOTHER BOOK!"

Give this one a try and see if you agree.

(If not, you're probably an adult!)

JIMMY PATTERSON BOOKS
FOR YOUNG READERS

James Patterson Presents
Sci-Fi Junior High by John Martin and Scott Seegert
Sci-Fi Junior High: Crash Landing by John Martin and Scott Seegert
How to Be a Supervillain by Michael Fry
How to Be a Supervillain: Born to Be Good by Michael Fry
How to Be a Supervillain: Bad Guys Finish First by Michael Fry
The Unflushables by Ron Bates
Ernestine, Catastrophe Queen by Merrill Wyatt

The Middle School Series by James Patterson
Middle School: The Worst Years of My Life
Middle School: Get Me Out of Here!
Middle School: Big Fat Liar
Middle School: How I Survived Bullies, Broccoli, and Snake Hill
Middle School: Ultimate Showdown
Middle School: Save Rafe!
Middle School: Just My Rotten Luck
Middle School: Dog's Best Friend
Middle School: Escape to Australia
Middle School: From Hero to Zero
Middle School: Born to Rock

The I Funny Series by James Patterson
I Funny
I Even Funnier
I Totally Funniest
I Funny TV
I Funny: School of Laughs
The Nerdiest, Wimpiest, Dorkiest I Funny Ever

The House of Robots Series by James Patterson
House of Robots
House of Robots: Robots Go Wild!
House of Robots: Robot Revolution

For exclusives, trailers, and other information,
visit jimmypatterson.org.

KATT vs. DOGG

JAMES PATTERSON
and CHRIS GRABENSTEIN

Illustrated by Anuki López

JIMMY PATTERSON BOOKS
LITTLE, BROWN AND COMPANY
New York Boston London

Copyright © 2019 by James Patterson
Illustrations copyright © 2019 by Anuki López

JIMMY Patterson Books / Little, Brown and Company
Hachette Book Group
1290 Avenue of the Americas, New York, NY 10104
JimmyPatterson.org

First Edition: April 2019

JIMMY Patterson Books is an imprint of Little, Brown and Company, a division of Hachette Book Group, Inc. The Little, Brown name and logo are trademarks of Hachette Book Group, Inc. The JIMMY Patterson Books® name and logo are trademarks of JBP Business, LLC.

Library of Congress Cataloging-in-Publication Data

Names: Patterson, James, 1947- author. | Grabenstein, Chris, author. | López, Anuki, illustrator.
Title: Katt vs. Dogg / James Patterson and Chris Grabenstein; illustrated by Anuki Lopez.
Other titles: Katt versus Dogg | Cat vs. Dog
Description: First edition. | New York: Little, Brown and Company, 2019 | "JIMMY Patterson Books." | Summary: A Dogg family and a Katt family are spending their vacations at Western Frontier Park fighting with each other when a youngster from each family becomes lost in the dangerous forest.
Identifiers: LCCN 2018059697 | ISBN 9780316411561 (alk. paper)
Subjects: | CYAC: Cats—Fiction. | Dogs—Fiction. | National parks and reserves—Fiction. | Imaginary creatures—Fiction. | Cooperativeness—Fiction. | Friendship—Fiction.
Classification: LCC PZ7.P27653 Kat 2019 | DDC [Fic]—dc23
LC record available at https://lccn.loc.gov/2018059697

10 9 8 7 6 5 4 3 2 1

LSC-H

Printed in the United States of America

For Parker and Phoebe Squeak
(katts) and in memory of Buster
and Fred (doggs)
—CG

Chapter 1

Oscar hung his head out the window of his father's pickup truck, his tongue flapping in the breeze. It was his favorite thing!

Oscar watched the wind sling his stringy slobber sideways. It was his favorite thing!

The truck was going seventy, maybe eighty miles an hour, swerving around all the other cars and trucks and motorcycles. Oscar saw shiny hubcaps spinning everywhere! He wanted to chase them all. Because chasing stuff was his favorite thing!

Oscar knew that this family vacation to the Western Frontier Park was going to be awesome because the ride to the park already was. It was his favorite road trip, ever!

Suddenly, Oscar heard something wet go *splat!* His father growled behind the wheel.

"Aw, cheese on a biscuit! One of them stupid katts in that stupid SUV just stuck out its stupid head and hocked up a hairball. It splatted all over my windshield here!"

"Duke?" said Oscar's mom. "Did you forget to take your distemper shot this morning?"

"No, Lola..."

"Because this was supposed to be a *fun* family vacation and—"

Splat!

Another wet gob of slimy hair coated with crud hit the windshield.

"Aww, bully stick!" grumbled Oscar's dad. "Why can't they just burp for once?" He jammed his paw down on the accelerator. The truck shot up the road even faster. "But nooooo...they always got to hock up *two* hairballs." He put on a funny,

3

fancy-pants katt voice. "'Oooh. Look at me. I'm so special! I'm a katt. Every time I puke, I puke twice...'"

"And they have to do that stupid thing where they heave their shoulders up and down first," added Fifi, Oscar's teenage sister. "Then they go 'gack-gack-gack.' Like they have to *announce* that they're going to puke or whatever. Katts are so totally gross and disgusting."

"So let's give them something to *really* puke about!" growled Dad. He pressed his paw down harder on the accelerator.

The rambling truck roared and rattled and raced up the road.

"Duke?" yelped Oscar's mom, holding on to an overhead handle for dear life. "You're scaring me!"

"Then sit on a wee-wee pad, Lola. Because a dogg's gotta do what a dogg's gotta do. I'm chasing that katt!"

Oscar gave that a hearty howl! "Aaaa-ooooh!"

The dusty pickup zoomed up the highway, cutting in and out of traffic, until it was parallel with the sleek black SUV.

"Hey, Mister Whiskers?" Dad shouted across the front seat to the katt behind the wheel. "Watch where you're pukin'!"

Oscar panted in happy anticipation. This was going to be so, so good.

Listening to his father yell at katts was his *favorite* favorite thing!

Chapter 2

Molly Hissleton sat in the backseat of her family's SUV, pretending to enjoy the classical music her father was listening to on the radio.

Molly was an excellent actress. She was good at pretending things.

The brand-new, fully equipped SUV (it had a litter box behind the backseat) hummed along the highway contentedly, its motor softly purring.

"Isn't Meowzart marvelous?" said Molly's father, as he conducted the symphonic music with synchronized flicks of his tail.

Molly's mother was curled up in the sunny front seat, napping peacefully. Molly's brother, Blade—who was feeling better after a brief bout of carsickness, which included some hairball hurling—was playing with his handheld game gizmo, chasing a red dot.

The katts were on their way to Western Frontier Park, home of rare, exotic, and frightfully wild creatures. Molly couldn't wait. It promised to be quite an extraordinary, dramatic vacation.

Suddenly, a rattly old pickup truck filled with slobbering doggs (yuck) pulled alongside the katts' sports utility vehicle. The curly furred mop in the passenger seat was covering her eyes with both paws while the snarling dogg behind the wheel barked something fierce. Of course, Molly couldn't hear what he was barking. The SUV had very good soundproofing.

There was a young dogg, a boy about Molly's age, with his head hanging out of the rear cab window. The boy was slobbering all over himself. So disgusting.

A fuzzy tennis ball bounced off the SUV driver's

side window. Molly rolled her eyes. Doggs were forever tossing tennis balls!

Molly's father sighed and powered down his tinted window. Molly glanced at the speedometer. They were flying along at eighty miles per hour! Molly sank her claws into the seat so she wouldn't get blown away.

"Yes?" her father sneered at the doggs through a sly grin. "Might I be of some assistance? Are you doggs looking for yet another place to pee?"

"Pull over!" barked the dogg behind the wheel.

"Oh, my," said Molly's father in the snarky way that always made her giggle. "Listen to the dogg using his words. *Both* of them."

"I know more words than them two!" shouted the dogg.

"Oh, really? Then speak, sir. Speak! I'm all ears. No, wait. That's your son. Except where he's all tongue, of course!"

"You want some of this?" shouted the driver dogg, shaking a balled-up paw at Molly's father.

"Some of what?" he replied. "Your dogg breath? Kindly chew a Milk-Bone before your next public speaking engagement, sir. Your beef jerky breath is stinking up the highway!"

"I'm going to stink you up, katt!"

"Is everything okay, Boomer, darling?" asked Molly's mom as she stretched and yawned in the passenger seat.

"Yes, Fluffy, dear. Go back to sleep. Just attempting to teach this old dogg a new trick."

"Good luck with that." She re-curled her body and fell fast asleep.

"Are we there yet?" asked Blade, looking up momentarily from his video game.

"No," said Molly. "Father's dealing with a dogg."

"I hate doggs," said Blade.

"Yes, Blade," said Molly. "We're katts. Hating doggs is what we do. Always have, always will."

Molly's father hissed at the doggs, showing his sharp teeth.

The doggs barked ferociously.

The katts meowed merrily.

Then Molly's father pushed the gas pedal to the floor, shot up the road like a rocket, and left the doggmobile behind in a cloud of dust and fumes.

"Doggs," chuckled Molly's father. "The more they bark, the less I care."

"Um, Father?" said Molly, looking out the rear window.

"Yes, dumpling?"

"The doggs. They're gaining on us!"

Chapter 3

The two vehicles screeched through the front gates of the Western Frontier Park in a cloud of smoke and a shower of sparks at exactly the same second!

Oscar's dad bounded out of the pickup truck, wagging his tail.

"Woof-hoo! In your face, katt! We beat you!"

"Woof-iddy-doo-dah!" yelped Oscar. "My dad's the best. Oh, yes, he is. Yes, he is!"

The katt driver slowly slinked out of the SUV, daintily licking his right paw as if he didn't have a

care in the whole, wide world.

"In what alternative universe does losing equal winning, flea brain?" he asked.

"Who are you calling flea brain, hairball?"

"If the stupid fits, wear it."

"Well, at least I don't smell like a can of tuna that's been sitting in the sun too long."

"No, you smell like a wet dogg. What's the matter? Couldn't wait till you found a fire hydrant?"

"What about you? Still peeing in a sandbox and trying to cover it up?"

"Enough!" shrieked the commanding voice of a majestic-looking hawkowl who was wearing a park ranger uniform and riding a horse with antlers.

"Wow!" said Oscar. "He's part hawk, part owl!"

"Yes," whispered his mother. "This park is filled with many magical and mythical creatures."

"Bunch of weirdos," whispered Oscar's dad out of the side of his muzzle. "He looks like a freak."

"I'm a she," said the hawkowl. "And thanks to my owl half, I have a highly developed auditory system."

"Huh?" said Oscar's father.

"She said she can hear very, very well, you dumb dogg!" shouted the katt driver as the rest of his family piled out of the SUV to preen in the sunshine. Except the teenage katt boy. He was playing a video game and stayed inside the car.

"Are we there yet?" he yowled.

"Yes, Blade."

"Then let's leave. I'm bored!"

"Can you soar like a hawk, ma'am?" Oscar

asked the park ranger eagerly (which is how he asked everything).

The hawkowl nodded. "Best of both species. I'm hawk-eyed and owl-eared."

"His horse is weird, too," Oscar's dad muttered. "Whoever heard of a horse with antlers?"

"Me," said the hawkowl. "As I said, I have *very* good hearing."

Chapter 4

My ancestors, you see," said the wise hawkowl, tucking her wings behind her back, "realized something you katts and doggs have failed to learn: The world is filled with many fierce and wild creatures, especially here on the far edge of civilization."

The dogg family tilted their heads sideways to listen.

The katts shut their eyes and yawned.

"Bor-r-r-ring," whined Blade.

The hawkowl kept going. "My ancestors quickly

Danger lurks around every corner in the wilderness. Beware the wild things! They're hungry 24/7.

realized that, up against the ferocious beasts who still roam the dark forests of this wilderness, they must, somehow, learn to live together or they would surely die alone."

"And that," Oscar's dad whispered snidely, "is how you end up with a freak show riding a moosehorse."

The doggs panted out a "heh-heh" chuckle.

"I can still hear you," said the hawkowl, tapping the side of her owl head with the tip of her hawk wing. "Good ears. Remember?"

20

"Whatever," muttered Fifi, who, like many teenagers, grew impatient whenever boring old people spoke wisely.

"Tell us when you're done, park person," said the tubby tabby, Blade. "We're missing our naps."

"Where, pray tell, is the katt section?" asked the katt mom. "We all need to bathe."

"You mean lick yourselves!" shouted Oscar's dad.

Oscar howled with laughter.

The hawkowl sighed. "'Oh, East is East and West is West, and never the twain shall meet.'"

"Huh?" said Oscar's dad.

"It's poetry," said the snobby katt dad, as his family climbed back into their SUV. "Read a book sometime!"

"Why read 'em when you can chew 'em?" said Oscar's dad, leading the way back into the pickup truck.

Oscar hopped into the backseat and stuck his head out the window again.

"What a shame," he heard the hawkowl lament to her moosehorse. "What a waste of our beautiful

21

park. The enmity between your two species has caused this world so much grief. Who can forget the saga of the doggs dumping kattnip into Pawston Harbor? Or the horrible Battle of Pettysburg during Furred War One? All creatures, great and small, have suffered because this enduring katt and dogg feud will never, ever end."

That made Oscar so happy he wagged his tail.

He was glad doggs and katts would never live together in peace.

He didn't want to ever use a litter box or chase red laser dots. Katts were dumb and there was no way he would ever feel different about them!

Chapter 5

Every morning, for the next five days, Oscar did the exact same thing.

Because doggs like routine.

Bright and early, before the rest of the family had even crawled out of their dogg beds, Oscar would bound out of his tent and give the air a good long sniff.

Delicious.

Dew mixed with clover with a hint of pine, sassafras, and mud.

"This park is paradise!" he exclaimed, checking

out the green fields and rolling hills and deep, deep forests and distant mountains. His tail was wagging to the right, which is the way it always wagged when he was happy. If it flapped to the left first that meant he was scared. But there was nothing to be scared about in the Western Frontier Park, no matter what that freaky old park ranger said. "So many sticks to fetch! So many fields to romp through! So many places to poop!"

And the best part about the dogg camp?

No katts. They had their own separate campground, thank you very much. It was way off,

somewhere in the east. There wasn't a scratching post or dangling thing or a bag of kattnip to be seen for miles. Just doggs and tennis balls and squeaky chew toys and bacon for breakfast and an awesome looking obstacle course for all the doggs who liked shepherding stuff. Oscar hadn't seen a katt for five full days, thank goodness!

Off in the distance, Oscar could see a mountain that looked like a huge hooked nose with a droopy wart on one side. Or maybe it looked like a pile of mashed potatoes with some kibble stuck into its peak. Or maybe it was a mountain made entirely out of chopped meat with a bone-shaped dogg biscuit poking out of the side.

Yes, he was definitely hungry. Time for a dogg's breakfast.

He pranced across the open field, heading to the mess hall, which, because it was for doggs, was always very messy. As he drew closer, he could smell sausage on top of the bacon. And a fresh bag of beef jerky that the chef had just ripped open with his teeth! He picked up his pace and broke into a trot.

Oscar was quite athletic. He was the star player on his school's tennis ball team. He was speedy, too. An average dogg can run about twenty miles per hour. Oscar? Coach clocked him doing twenty-seven! He was also pretty agile. He might have to try out that obstacle course after breakfast and then, of course, reward himself with a nap.

He was just about to dash into the mess hall and stick his muzzle in a bowl of meaty mush when he had to dig in his rear paws and skid to a stop—or he would've crashed into a sleek, black SUV.

The same SUV that they'd chased into the park the day they arrived!

Chapter 6

It was the same supersnooty katt family!

Oscar sat down and tilted his head to the right while the katt dad scampered down out of the SUV.

Their eyes met.

The hair and hackles on Oscar's back shot up.

The katt dad hissed. "Trust me," he said to Oscar with disdain. "I don't want to be here amidst you mangy mutts and mongrels, either!"

Oscar tilted his head an inch more to the right. He didn't really know what "amidst" meant. Plus, there wasn't a mist anywhere. No fog, either.

The katt clawed a long gouge into a fence post. When he made a splinter of jagged wood stick out, he used it like a nail to hang a sign.

It was a Missing Katt poster.

MISSING KATT

FIND MOLLY TODAY!!!!

WHITE FUR, BLUE EYES, LAST SEEN CHASING A BUTTERFLY

Huh, thought Oscar. *Why bother looking for a lost katt?*

Would anybody in the whole world miss one measly katt?

There seemed to be a billion of them running around scaring birds, tormenting mice, and yowling at the moon. One less wouldn't matter.

Plus, Oscar was on vacation. Doggs didn't hunt for lost stuff on vacation. Except bacon. If a slab of bacon went missing, then every dogg in the park would form a search party, sniff the ground, and track it down.

The katt dad climbed back into his SUV,

muttering, "Waste of a sign. Doggs can't read. If they could, they'd beware of themselves, just like all the signs say!"

The tires on the big black vehicle shot gravel backward as it sped away.

When it stopped blocking the mess hall entrance, Oscar could, once again, savor the delish aroma of bacon grease mixed with sausage grease. He licked his chops. It was breakfast time.

"Oscar!"

Uh-oh. His tail wagged to the left.

Because his dad was screaming his name, which was still scary, even though his dad basically screamed all the time.

"Come here, boy!" said his dad. "Grab your backpack. Your mother says we need to go on a nature hike this morning."

Oh, boy, thought Oscar. We're heading off into the glorious, magical, marvelous park!

He loped over to where his dad, mom, and sister were waiting.

"What about breakfast?" he asked eagerly (like always).

His mother smiled. "I packed meat loaf sandwiches and bacon smoothies."

Oh, boy, thought Oscar.

Meat loaf sandwiches and bacon smoothies were his favorites!

Chapter 7

Oscar slung his knapsack onto his back.

"Did you hear?" he said to his dad. "One of those katts we met on our first day here is missing!"

"Good," said his father. "One less for me to chase up a tree."

"Duke?" said Oscar's mom. "Honestly. We're on vacation."

"Maybe. But a true dogg's hatred of katts never takes a day off."

"Totally," said Fifi. "They're, like, so prissy. And

cheesy. Their butts smell like cheese."

"Cheese?" said Oscar. "Is there cheese on the meat loaf sandwiches?"

"Yes, dear," said his mother. "Peanut butter, too."

"Oh boy, oh boy, oh boy!"

Drool slobbered down the front of his shirt. His mother didn't mind. She was drooling, too. All the doggs were. It's what doggs do.

They hiked up a trail lined with pine bark mulch.

"This really is a magical place," said Oscar's mom, enjoying the scenery.

Birds chirped. Butterflies fluttered. Bees buzzed. A rainbow appeared in the sky even though it hadn't rained. Water cascaded over a fall, sending up a very refreshing cloud of cool mist. The air was fragrant with the scent of wildflowers.

Everything was in perfect harmony.

Which meant, after about an hour, it was also kind of boring.

Oscar could only take so much perfection and magic. He needed action. Adventure. Speed!

He was also easily distracted.

Especially when a flying squirrel zoomed from one evergreen tree to another.

"Oh, boy!" cried Oscar. "Squirrel! Flying squirrel! They're my favorite."

He took off running. Fast!

Chapter 8

Oscar flew through the underbrush as the squirrel flew through the canopy of trees overhead.

"I'm going to get you, you nutty squirrel!" Oscar shouted. "I'm fast! Fastest player on my tennis ball team."

"You're not faster than me!" chirped the flying squirrel, drifting effortlessly through the air. He had a very squeaky voice. "I'm just gliding, here, pal! Not even breaking a sweat. This is so easy, I'm nibbling the nuts I've had stored in my cheeks since last winter. *Nom, nom, nom.* Delish."

Oscar snorted the scent of the flying squirrel deep into his nostrils and stored the smell away in his brain. Now, even if he couldn't see the squirrel, he could still chase it.

"I'm going to get you!" Oscar gloated with glee.

"You said that already," chittered the squirrel, twenty feet overhead.

"Well, I'm going to. Oh, yes I am."

"Oh, no, you're not!" scoffed the squirrel as it floated between trees like an autumn leaf with a jet pack. "You're on the ground, pal. I'm in the air."

"I can jump!"

"Fine, pal. Jump. And while you do that, I think I'll—oh, I don't know—fly away!"

Oscar splashed across a shallow creek as the squirrel leapt from one tree to the next, spreading out its arms and legs to stretch its skin into a sail.

Oscar's shirt was sopping wet. His pants were splattered with mud.

"This is fun!" he huffed.

"Fun?" laughed the squirrel. "Ha! You're nuttier than the port-a-potty at my last family reunion!"

"So? Chasing squirrels is my favorite thing!"

"You need a new hobby, buddy!"

"My name's not Buddy. Buddy's my uncle. I'm Oscar! And I can run twenty-seven miles an hour!"

The squirrel kept soaring.

Oscar kept running.

Two hours later, the sun started setting. Oscar couldn't see the squirrel against the darkening sky, but he could still smell it. So he kept running. For another hour.

In his head, he did the math.

"I've been running twenty-seven miles an hour for three hours. That means I've run...uh...really, really far."

In fact, he'd run so far, he had no idea where he was.

Oscar was totally and completely lost.

Chapter 9

*O*opsie, thought Oscar.

He put on the brakes. His tail wagged. Then it sagged between his hind legs. He was scared.

No, terrified. He'd never ever been lost before. Being lost was *not* one of his favorite things.

"Oh, what's the matter, pal?" chirped the annoying flying squirrel from a high branch in a tall tree. "Run out of gas? I thought you were doggedly determined to catch me. See what I did there? I made a pun. You want another one? I once knew a dogg who wasn't fat, he was just a little husky. Get it? Husky?"

"Help," Oscar yipped.

"Sorry, pal. Couldn't hear you up here."

"Help!" Oscar shouted.

Then, he started barking it and baying it and howling it and yowling it!

"Help, help, help, help!"

He wailed for help so hard for so long, his throat started to hurt.

"Whoa!" chirped the chattering squirrel from its perch in the tree. "Give it a rest, why don't you? Can't nobody hear you because there ain't nobody in this part of the park except a few squirrels, a couple birds, and, oh, yeah—a bunch of wild carnivorous beasts. Not for nothin', but carnivorous means they like to eat meat. Dogg meat, katt meat—they ain't particular."

Oscar started to panic. "Help, help, help, help, help!"

"You're so dumb, dogg," laughed the squirrel. "You probably sit on the TV to watch the couch."

Oscar had heard enough. He was going to catch that darn squirrel.

He jumped as high as he could. About twice his length.

Oscar couldn't jump as well as he could run. In fact, he barely reached the first branch. The squirrel, who was probably part katt, was way up in the twentieth or thirtieth limb. Oscar couldn't count that high. He still wasn't very good at math.

He decided to abandon his flying squirrel quest and try to find his way back to the dogg camp.

He trotted about fifty yards and came to a burbling stream trickling across a path of rocks that made excellent stepping stones.

Oscar crossed the creek—one rock at a time—then headed up into the forest. After maybe a quarter of a mile, he took a right turn at a moss-covered boulder, ran maybe another quarter of a mile, scampered down a steep slope, leapt across a narrow waterfall, hurried downstream on the far bank, turned left at a gnarled stump, right at a grass clump, then left, right, left, right until he came to a burbling stream trickling across a path of rocks that made excellent stepping stones.

He was right back where he had started.

And now the sun was completely gone. The sky was black and filled with tiny, twinkling stars. The only sounds were the creak of crickets and the soft hoot of owls.

Oscar had never been this alone before.

He was a city dogg lost in the woods—somewhere on the far edge of civilization.

His ears were back, his head bowed, and his tail was tucked tightly between his haunches.

This was not good. This was the opposite of good.

This was like when he was a puppy and used to pee on the rug in the house.

This was bad, bad, bad.

Chapter 10

But Oscar had one thing going for him. He was a determined and dedicated Dogg Scout.

Plus, he still had his backpack! And he was close enough to the creek that he didn't have to worry about water. He could lap it straight from the stream. Which he did. For five whole minutes.

Then, paws trembling slightly, he gathered up all the kindling and broken branches he could find circling the bases of the tall trees. Stacking his wood, crisscross style, inside a circle of stones, he found the waterproof tube of wooden matches he always carried (because a Dogg Scout is Always Prepared) and, in no time, he'd made a nice, cozy fire.

Now he had warmth. And light. And the crackling pop of burning wood to drown out all the hoot owls and other spooky forest noises in the night.

"Time for supper!" Oscar said to no one in particular because he was alone.

He rummaged around in his knapsack. He didn't find any meat loaf sandwiches wrapped in wax paper (Mom always carried those in her picnic hamper) but he did find three cans of dogg food. He popped open the one labeled BEEF AND GRAVY and poured it into his tin camping bowl. It looked delish.

Of course, Oscar was so hungry, anything would look delish. Even mashed dirt.

He stuck his face in the bowl and gobbled down his dinner.

Still hungry, he thought about opening another can.

No, he thought. *Save it for breakfast.*

But then, he had another thought. *Both cans?*

You don't need two cans of dogg food for breakfast. So you can have one for dessert and—

He stopped thinking.

Because, suddenly, the woods surrounding him were filled with scary noises and frightening scents.

And eyes. Lots and lots of glowing eyes.

One pair of eyeballs stepped out of the darkness and turned into a huge mountain lion!

Shoulders rolling, it prowled forward on padded feet.

The huge mountain lion wasn't wearing any clothes! And it was walking on all four paws! That meant it was some kind of wild beast. The first one Oscar had ever seen.

The mountain lion crept closer.

It skulked right past him.

Right. Past. Him.

Then it stopped, turned around, and growled in Oscar's face.

Whoa. Wild or not, the mountain lion definitely needed to brush its fangs more often. Its breath smelled like a pound of hamburger that'd been stored for a month in an ice chest without any ice.

"Hello, dogg," the fierce mountain lion whispered in a hiss. "My, my, my. You certainly are a tempting little morsel, aren't you? Too bad I already ate my supper. But, then again, there's always breakfast! Not quite certain what might be on the menu tomorrow morning. Dogg, squirrel, porcupine, muskrat. So many choices. Why, it's a veritable breakfast buffet in this neck of the woods. See you at dawn, lost little boy."

The wild beast wandered away, licking its chops.

Oscar started frantically digging a hole so he could bury himself and hide.

Breakfast? First thing in the morning?

He'd never been more frightened in his life!

Chapter II

That same night, in the log lodge that served as the headquarters for the Western Frontier Park, the majestic hawkowl ranger was holding an emergency meeting with the families of the missing dogg, Oscar, and the missing katt, Molly.

The two families stood on opposite sides of the great room, growling and hissing at each other.

"Madam Ranger?" said Molly's father, Boomer. "Might we open a window or two? The dogg stench in this room is positively overpowering."

"Is that, so, kitty litter breath?" barked Oscar's

father, Duke. "All I smell is fish. What'd you fur-balls eat for dinner tonight? Soup made out of the ocean?"

"Silence!" demanded the hawkowl. "Your constant bickering, barking, and caterwauling isn't going to help us find Oscar and Molly, who, might I remind you, are both lost in the wilderness. And by wilderness I mean a dangerous and dark forest filled with *wild beasts*. The kind that don't pick up their meals at the supermarket! The kind that eat whatever smells good or happens to wander across their path."

Duke and Boomer both swallowed hard when the hawkowl said that. And then they both did something miraculous. They both shut up.

"Now then," said the hawkowl, ruffling up her chest feathers and pacing back and forth on her perch, "I wanted to let you know that I've called up our elite rescue squad. The finest hybrid hunters in the world: the grizzly wolfbears and the lionodiles."

Four enormous creatures decked out in rescue team gear marched into the meeting hall. The two grizzly wolfbears had the heads of wolves and the bodies of grizzly bears. The pair of lionodiles were half lion (the top) and half crocodile (the bottom).

"These creatures are combinations of nature's greatest hunters," said the hawkowl. "The two grizzly wolfbears will patrol the forests. The pair of lionodiles will search the park by swiftly swimming through its many waterways. My fellow hawkowls and I will provide air support and fly reconnaissance missions."

One of the lionodiles, who seemed to be the leader of the rescue team, stepped forward. "We will not return until we find your children," he proclaimed, shaking out his magnificent mane. "Even if it means getting my hair wet."

Boomer and Duke stepped forward to shake the lionodile's scaly hand.

"Thank you, good sir," said Boomer.

"Yeah," said Duke. "Thanks, pal."

The noble lionodile nodded. "I can only imagine how you two must feel right now. For I am a father, too."

When the rescue team leader said that, all the two fathers could do was nod.

And sniffle.

And, when they were sure the other one wasn't watching, they both sobbed.

Chapter 12

Meanwhile, off in the dark wilderness, Oscar heard a rustling in the woods.

And it was scarily close.

Deep in his hidey-hole, Oscar started to shake all over—and not just because he was cold (his campfire had burned out and he was too terrified to search in the darkness for more wood).

It's the mountain lion, he thought. *It's come back for a midnight snack. Me!*

More rustling. Twigs snapping. Leaves softly crunching.

Wait a second. A new thought flitted across Oscar's brain. *Softly crunching? That mountain lion was HUGE. It couldn't softly crunch anything if it tried.*

Mustering all the courage he could (it wasn't much; his courage batteries were nearly drained), Oscar poked his head up an inch and peered over the lip of his hastily dug hole.

He did, indeed, see a katt. But it wasn't the mountain lion, distant cousin to all the katts who lived in the city of Kattsburgh. No, it was a young girl. Maybe his own age. When she stepped into the moonlight, Oscar could see that she had white fur (well, it was kind of off-white because it was seriously matted and full of leaves, dirt, and twigs). Her blue eyes sparkled like the ones in a stuffed toy katt that Oscar chewed through once.

The katt was also missing the tip of her tail and the top of one ear.

What in the name of tug toys happened to her? Oscar wondered.

He stuck his head up a little higher. When he did, his metal Dogg Scout neckerchief clasp dinged against a rock. It pinged like a high-

pitched bell. The katt's ears shot up.

She saw Oscar and hissed.

So Oscar did what any other dogg in his situation would do.

He chased after the katt!

Chapter 13

Molly sighed once and then bolted away from the dumb dogg's ridiculous excuse for a campsite.

Typical dogg, she thought. *Forgets all about the ferocious mountain lion prowling around out here and chases after me, instead! Dad is right: doggs are dumb with a capital D.*

"You're just like my brother!" Molly shouted over her shoulder. "So easily distracted! You have the attention span of a gnat!"

"Yeah," said the dogg from ten yards back. "I

sometimes worry about that. But not for long. I'm going to get you, katt! Oh, yes I am."

Molly ran with her head level. The dogg's head, of course, would be bobbing up and down. Easier for the drool to drip off his flopping tongue while he panted.

"I can smell you!" barked the dogg.

"Oh, really?" said Molly, darting sideways into the underbrush. "I could smell *you* from two miles away. You smell like a wet, dirty dogg!"

Molly was swift and had more moves than the dogg. But, she had to admit, the dogg was fast. He was right on her tail and gaining!

Molly wasn't really sure why she had ventured toward the dogg's hiding place. Maybe because she hadn't seen another civilized creature for a while. Not since she snuck off into the woods to work on her emoting skills and ended up getting lost.

Horribly, terribly, miserably lost.

Molly wanted to be an actress. Actresses had to show a wide range of emotions, something that was difficult for most katts. They usually went from cuddly to snarky and vicious without much in between.

Her father and mother didn't approve of Molly's dreams of being on the stage or, better yet, in the movies. Some katts made excellent actresses and performers, like Kattalie Portman and Kitty Purry. In fact, Molly's favorite films all featured katts: *The Fast and the Fur-ious, Whiskers in the Dark, Kitty Kitty Bang Bang*. But Molly was a good girl. She always did what her mother and father told her to do. At least when they were watching.

"Waste of time," her father had purred when she told him her dreams of being an actress. "Trained doggs appear in shows for other people's entertainment. Sensible katts appear only when they want to."

"Concentrate on your napping, dear," suggested her mother. "It's the only skill you'll ever need."

"Plus bathing," her father would always add. "Mustn't forget bathing. Feline hygiene is very important." And then he'd sit down and lick himself.

But Molly wanted more.

Of course, at that very instant, all she really wanted was to get away from the stupid boy dogg charging after her!

Fine, she thought. *This dogg and katt chase will end as dogg and katt chases have ended since time immemorial.*

She spotted a tree with two trunks split like a V and leapt nimbly between them.

The dogg?

He was once again easily distracted. He saw a fluttering moth and stopped watching where he was going.

That's when he banged his muzzle right into one of the tree trunks!

Chapter 14

Holding his sore nose, which made it hard to sniff for directions, Oscar eventually found his way back to his meager campsite.

"Stupid katt. Made me chase her," he muttered. "Stupid moth. Made me chase him, too."

All the late-night running had really worked up Oscar's appetite.

"Guess I'll go ahead and eat another can of dogg food," he said aloud, because the night noises in the forest were so creepy. It was comforting to hear a sound he recognized: his own voice.

He went to his knapsack.

"What the...?"

Its canvas had been ripped to shreds, as if someone had torn into it with their claws.

It was also empty. Oscar turned the backpack upside down and shook it.

Nothing fell out.

"I had two cans of dogg food and a rawhide stick!" he howled at the moon.

Then Oscar realized the horrible truth: He *was* too easily distracted. And while he was distracted chasing after that sneaky white katt, she had, somehow, snuck back to the campsite and stolen his food!

"Aw, barf me a biscuit!" he moaned. "I hate katts! Especially the ones with blue eyeballs and white fur who steal your dogg food! I'd like to bury that katt in a dirty litter box!"

"Ha!" someone laughed out in the woods. "My litter box is never dirty. I scoop it on a regular basis. A katt is nothing if it is not clean. That's what my father says."

Drat! thought Oscar. *It was the katt!* The one

he'd chased. He could see her blue eyeballs glowing in the dark.

"Plus," taunted the katt, "before you could do anything to me you'd have to catch me. And, given your proclivity for stupidly running into trees, the chances of that ever happening are—oh, I don't know—zip or maybe zilch."

"Go away, katt," Oscar whined. "You stole my food!"

"Did not."

"Did, too!"

"Not!"

"Did!"

The katt laughed. "Why would I steal your dogg food, dogg?"

"Because you were hungry."

"Ha! There's never been a katt alive who was so hungry they'd eat that slop."

"It wasn't Slopp brand dogg food. It was Chunkee Stuff! And it's delish. Now go away."

"Sorry. We katts are nocturnal. Means we stay up all night. And since there's nothing good on TV this late—not to mention no TV out here in the trees—I decided I'd just hang out up here and watch you being miserable. It's highly entertaining."

"Go away!"

"Oh, look," cried the katt. "The clouds just parted. The moon is full! Meowww!"

"Knock it off!"

"Sorry. No can do. It's instinctual. We see a moon, we howl at it. Meeeooowww!"

Oscar covered his ears.

"Meooooow!"

He hated that horrible noise katts could make. So, to drown it out, he started barking.

It was useless. Probably pointless, too.

But, somehow, barking made Oscar feel a little better.

Anything he could do to annoy that annoying katt made Oscar happy!

Chapter 15

At sunrise the next morning, down at the Western Frontier Park, the head park ranger was perched on her moosehorse, meeting with the distraught katt and dogg families.

"Our night flights found no sign of either child," she reported.

"Did you use your night vision?" asked Molly's father, Boomer.

"Always," said the hawkowl. "Comes with being part owl."

"How about campfires?" asked Duke. "Our

Oscar's a Dogg Scout. He knows how to build a fire."

"Oh, joy," said Boomer. "Just what our sweet little Molly needs while she's lost in the forest primeval. A pyromaniac mutt running around the woods playing with matches!"

"Oscar's a good boy!" said his mother. "He doesn't play with matches."

"Are you sure he wouldn't have trouble reading the instructions on the matchbook?" sniffed Fluffy, Molly's mother. "That whole 'close cover, strike match' thing a little too complicated for him?"

"Silence," commanded the hawkowl. "We saw no signs of campfires, either. However, at this time of year, the forest canopy is at its thickest. We can't spy everything on the ground."

"I thought you were like a hawk," said Oscar's sister, Fifi, snidely.

"Yeah," said Molly's brother, Blade. "Aren't you supposed to be, like, hawk-eyed?"

"I am!" said the hawkowl, her feathers ruffling slightly. "But, ladies and gentlemen, boys and girls, the Western Frontier Park is huge. Seven hundred and fifty thousand acres."

Duke whistled. "Impressive."

"Indeed," added Boomer. "Quite a spread."

"Wouldn't want to mow it," said Blade.

"Or mark it," said Fifi.

The hawkowl ignored them all.

"It would be impossible," she said, "to cover every square inch in a single night. Let's just pray that your son and your daughter use their common sense and stay put. It's much easier to find a missing person if they don't make our job more difficult by moving around."

"We're ready to head out, chief," said the lead grizzly wolfbear, pointing to his team.

"One moment, please," said Boomer, holding up a paw and shooting out a single claw. "Aren't you related to the dogg family?"

"I beg your pardon?" said the wolfbear.

"You're part wolf," said Boomer. "Wolves are related to doggs."

"And your point is?"

"Simple. You'll show favoritism. You'll find

their dogg son before you even start looking for our katt daughter."

"No, sir. That's not how it works. We search. We rescue. And we do it without fear or favoritism!"

"Hoo-ah!" cried an army of searchers as they marched forward out of the forest.

Some were grizzly wolfbears. Others were lion-odiles, paddling in the stream that wound its way past the park headquarters. Others were volunteers—families of pigs, hamsters, rabbits (those were very large families), cows, sheep, plus every other animal in the land—all of them willing to sacrifice their own family vacations in the park to help the katts and doggs find their missing children.

"You see how everyone else is pitching in?" asked the hawkowl, as she observed the army of volunteers. "How they're willing to give up their own vacations to help us find Molly and Oscar?"

"Indeed," said Boomer.

"I guess," said Duke.

"Well, then," said the hawkowl, "surely you two could, temporarily, set aside your historical differences and work together for the common good?"

The katts and doggs stared at the hawkowl.

For maybe a minute.

And then they exploded.

"What? Are you kidding? Help a katt?"

"Lend a paw to a dogg? No, way, feather brain."

All the hawkowl could do was roll her eyes.

And hope the rescue parties found the two missing children before their parents killed each other.

Chapter 16

Oscar didn't sleep well at all.

A katt yowling at the moon all night long will do that to a dogg.

And, since the blue-eyed katt had stolen his last two cans of Chunkee Stuff dogg food, he was still starving. His stomach was growling so loudly he was afraid the mountain lion might hear it.

Uh-oh. He'd almost forgotten. It was morning, which meant it was breakfast time. And Oscar might be the main course on the lion's menu!

He quickly stirred the ashes in his charred fire

pit with a wet stick to make sure there weren't any glowing embers that might spark a forest fire. A good Dogg Scout always checked for glowing embers before abandoning a campsite.

He looked inside the pockets of his torn backpack, searching for his compass.

Gone.

So was his waterproof match holder.

"That kleptomaniac katt stole everything!" he muttered. But he didn't have time to stand around a cold fire pit muttering. He had to keep moving. He had to find his way out of this forest.

Of course, he had absolutely no clue about how to do that.

So, he just took off. Randomly running through the thick brambles and brush.

Actually, he was trotting. And then jogging. Finally, he was strolling because the underbrush was so thick there was no way for him to move through it without swatting green leafy branches out of his face every two seconds. He couldn't see more than a few feet in front of his snout. And all he could smell was green stuff. Leaves. More leaves. Different leaves. Spunk water in stumps.

But he kept moving forward.

Until he heard something behind him.

Twig snaps. Padded paws crushing soft dirt. A contented purr.

The mountain lion!

Slowly, very slowly, Oscar turned around.

"Hiya, dogg. Sleep well?"

It was the white katt with the sparkling blue eyes.

"Truce?" she said, extending a paw in what almost looked like friendship.

Oscar hesitated, for just a second, then remembered who he was. A dogg!

"Absolutely not, food thief," he told her.

"For the last time, dogg, I didn't steal your canned meat slop."

"Yeah, right. Everybody knows you katts are nothing but cunning little crooks and liars."

"No, we're not."

"See? There you go again. You're lying about being a liar!"

"Fine. Have it your way, kibble brains. Go ahead

and die out here all alone. See if I care."

She turned to walk away.

Oscar saw her nipped-off tail again and the one ear where the point had been tipped.

"Have fun being the breakfast buffet, soup bone," hissed the katt as she walked away. "I'm sure the mountain lion's going to love sinking its fangs into you!"

That made Oscar's eyes go wide. "Wait a second!" he barked.

The katt spun back around. "What?"

"How'd you know about the mountain lion?"

The katt frowned and pointed a paw at her tail.

"What do you think happened back here, dogg breath?"

Chapter 17

Molly realized she'd been lost in the woods for way too long.

It was making her brain fuzzy. Her mind mushy.

How else could she explain her attempt to do the impossible: have an intelligent conversation with a dogg? She was *soooo* glad her father wasn't there to see her behaving so ridiculously.

"The tip of my tail was nipped by a mountain lion," she said. "I told the big katt that it was an extremely rude thing for him to do, especially since, according to my zoology teacher, we're somehow related."

The dogg tilted his head sideways and had a confused look in his eyes.

"We're both katts," Molly tried to explain. "Me and the mountain lion. It'd be like if a wolf tried to eat you."

"There's a wild wolf out here, too?" yelped the dogg. "They're our cousins! They're kind of wild. It's why we never invite them to the family reunions."

"Same with us and the mountain lions."

"So if the mountain lion nipped your tail, then what happened to your ear?" the dogg asked.

"Fox," Molly answered with a shudder.

"My ancient ancestors used to hunt foxes," said the dogg, a little too eagerly. "They'd chase them all through the forest. I bet it was fun."

"Not if you're the one being chased by the fox," said Molly.

"Yeah. I guess not. Never had that happen to me. Guess I'm just a lucky dogg."

Molly nodded. She could use a little luck.

She could also use a traveling companion. She couldn't face another day alone in the forest with no one to talk to except the rocks and trees.

"I've been out here for ages," she said with a sigh. "Last night, I was so hungry..."

"You stole my food!"

Molly rolled her eyes. "No. Judging from the size of the claw marks on your backpack, I'd say the mountain lion ripped it to shreds."

She showed him her claws.

"Mine are much smaller. Daintier."

"Oh," said the dogg. "Sorry."

"I'm Molly," she said, turning around and flipping up her tail. "Want to sniff my butt?"

"No! I do not want to sniff your butt, katt!"

"Fine," said Molly. "Because I'm not going to rub up against your legs, which is how we katts introduce ourselves."

"Good," said the dogg. "You'd probably give me a rash. All doggs are allergic to katts."

"Look," said Molly, feeling exasperated. "We're both lost, correct?"

"Yeah. I guess. I mean I can't say for certain that I'm lost because I don't know where I am. So, I guess that means I *am* lost."

"Exactly! I think the two of us have a better chance of surviving out here in the wilderness if we, temporarily, for a limited time only, work together. Deal?"

"Why would I want to hang around with a katt? I'm supposed to hate you!"

Molly closed her bright-blue eyes for a moment. "Because we both want to get home to our families. And with mountain lions, foxes, no food, and no idea where we're going, we need to help each other."

Oscar looked around the dark, silent forest. "I guess," he said reluctantly.

"So, what's your name?"

"Oscar."

"I'm Molly."

"I know. You already told me."

"I thought you might've forgotten. It was two minutes ago."

"I'm not dumb, katt. In fact, doggs are some of the most intelligent creatures on the planet. You put peanut butter deep inside a hollow bone, we'll find a way to lick it out."

"Can you, uh, find some of that peanut butter now?"

"I'll put it on my list of things to sniff for."

"Thanks."

The two of them set off, neither one really knowing which way to go. They only knew they wouldn't be going there alone.

Chapter 18

Down at the Western Frontier Park, the news media was swarming all over the story of the two missing children.

The head park ranger appeared for a hastily arranged press conference.

"If anyone has any information as to the whereabouts of Oscar and Molly, please contact your local authorities. If you see something, screech something."

A ferret in a fedora pushed her way forward and jabbed her microphone into the hawkowl's beak.

"Have you found any evidence that these two children are still alive?" demanded the ferret.

"Yes," said the wise hawkowl. "In fact, this morning, a team of wolfbears came upon an abandoned campsite in the forest. We think that is where Oscar spent the night. There were dogg tracks leading down to the creek. We also found what we think are katt paw prints in the same general vicinity."

"If that dogg harms one whisker on my little girl's head, he'll answer to me!" hissed Molly's father, swatting the air with his extended claws.

"And you, sir, are?" asked the reporter, whipping her microphone over to the katt.

"Boomer Hissleton the Third, Esquire."

"Ah, go chase a ball of yarn, mackerel mouth!" snapped Oscar's dad.

"Take care, sir," said the katt, as he coolly assumed a karate stance. "You do not wish to anger me. I am quite proficient in the martial arts!"

"Ha! You think you scare me? You couldn't slice up a couch if it were made out of butter."

The ferret swung her microphone back and forth between the growling animals. "What is your relation to the missing katt and dogg, sirs?"

"These, unfortunately, are the missing children's fathers," said the hawkowl with intense scorn.

"Yo!" barked Oscar's dad, Duke. "Was that intense scorn I just heard in your voice, birdbrain?"

"I heard it, too," added Boomer.

"Yeah, well, I heard it first!"

Boomer shrugged. "You also eat socks!"

"So? *You're* afraid of water." Duke put on his snooty katt voice again. "Oh, look. A water bowl. I'm sooooo afraid!"

"At least I don't drink out of a toilet!"

Molly and Oscar's mothers and siblings leapt into the fray with hisses, howls, and spit. The news crews swung their microphones and cameras back and forth, trying to capture the frantic action.

"Ssssstupid doggsssss," said Blade, spewing Fifi with spittle. "Can't even keep their tonguesssss in their mouthssss."

"Say it, don't spray it," snapped Fifi.

"Enough!" cried the majestic hawkowl.

Her voice was commanding enough to silence all the doggs and all the katts.

"Regretfully," she declared, "I must hereby order both katt and dogg families to vacate this park, immediately."

"What?" said Oscar's mother.

"I beg your pardon?" said Molly's mom.

"Go. Home. Now!" said the hawkowl. "You are

of absolutely no help to us. In fact, your open hostility is making our rescue mission more difficult than it need be! Leave. If and when we find your children, we will return them to you so you can continue warping their young minds with ignorant hatred. The same thing you incorrigible creatures have done for centuries!"

The doggs and katts were stunned into silence.

The two moms started sobbing first. Blade and Fifi were next. They wailed and howled as only teenagers can. Finally, the two fathers wept manly dad tears.

"I can tell you love your missing kids," said the wise hawkowl, shaking her head. "But you katts and doggs are simply hopeless."

Chapter 19

Oscar couldn't believe he was hiking through the forest with a katt.

But, he figured he didn't have a choice. At least not until he was safely home, then he'd have all sorts of choices.

"This truce only lasts until we get back to base camp, right?" he said. "After that, I don't know you and you don't know me."

"Whatever," said Molly. "Let's head west."

Oscar grinned. He'd heard that katts could be

tricky. Sneaky, too. So, he'd do the exact opposite of whatever Molly suggested.

"Nope," he said. "We're going east."

"East? I've already been east. It's a waste of time. There's nothing there but a big cliff. I've seen it. Six different times!"

The katt knelt down on the trail and started scratching the dirt with her pointy claws. She gestured at Oscar's tattered uniform. "You're supposed to be a Dogg Scout, right?"

"Yes," Oscar said proudly. "I have fourteen merit badges. Most of them for chewing different things. Rope. Sticks. Squeak toys. Rawhide…"

"Well, let me draw you a map, Dogg Scout. East is the cliff. South, that's behind us, that's where the mountain lion likes to hang out."

Oscar nodded. He hated to admit it, but the katt was making sense.

"Okay, I've changed my mind," he announced. "We should go north or west."

"I choose west," said Molly.

"Sorry," said Oscar. "I don't really trust your

sense of direction. I, on the other hand, was a Dogg Scout. Obviously, I know more about what I'm doing than you do."

"Fine. Don't give yourself heartworms. We'll go north."

"Nope. West."

"West? That's what I said two minutes ago!"

"But I said it most recently. So, it's my idea."

Molly heaved a humongous sigh. "Fine. Whatever. Lead on."

Oscar trotted along the path, sniffing the breeze. No familiar scents tickled his nostrils.

After silently trudging through the wilderness, seeing nothing but trees and more trees, the two hikers finally came to a hilltop clearing.

"There!" Oscar panted. "That mountain! Way off in the distance! Do you see it?"

"Uh, yeah, Oscar," said Molly. "It's a mountain. Mountains are very hard *not* to see."

"I know that mountain!" said Oscar. "See how it looks like a huge hooked nose with a droopy wart on one side?"

"Yes," said Molly. "Sort of like your muzzle."

"That's not a wart on my muzzle," said Oscar, swiping his paw across his nose. "That's a booger. Anyway, I could see that exact same mountain from our campsite! It's what they call a landmark. Landmarks are good when you're lost. They mark the land for you!"

"Good work!" said Molly. "You're not as dumb as you look."

"Dumb? Hey, if I'm so dumb, how come I know

that katts have more than twenty muscles to control their ears? Too bad you don't have one to control your mouth!"

"Who studies katt muscles?" snarled the katt.

"A Dogg Scout working on his kattology merit badge, that's who!"

"Why would a dogg want to know so much about katts?"

Oscar didn't answer. His body went stiff. His eyes bugged out.

He raised one paw and pointed.

"Groundhog!"

And he took off running after it.

Chapter 20

Molly chased after the dogg who was chasing after a groundhog.

A naked groundhog. That meant it was one of the wild things living away from civilization.

"Did you get your rabies shot this year?" Molly hollered after Oscar. "Because if you didn't, that wild groundhog is going to give you one when it bites you in the butt! It's a wild creature, Oscar! Leave it alone."

"Can't," shouted Oscar. "It's a groundhog. I'm

a dogg. This is what they call instinct! A dogg's gotta do what a dogg's gotta do!"

"You're going to get us lost, again!" said Molly, trying to keep up with the dogg, who, she had to admit, was extremely athletic and could run very, very fast. "We're supposed to be hiking to the mountain. The one that's in the opposite direction of where you're chasing that groundhog!"

Just then, a flying squirrel flitted through the tree branches overhead.

"Squirrel!" shouted Oscar.

He dug in his paws, skidded to a stop, abandoned his wild groundhog chase, and took off after the flying squirrel.

"You are so like my brother!" cried Molly. "Blade would chase a reflection up a wall until he saw something shinier, and then he'd chase after that!"

"I have to chase squirrels!" shouted Oscar. "Just like you have to spend your day unrolling toilet paper and climbing into cardboard boxes."

"I don't do that kitten stuff," said Molly

defensively. "Because I am no ordinary katt. I'm studying to be an actress!"

"Great," said Oscar, still running. "Give me a few lessons and I'll act like I'm interested."

He slammed on his brakes again.

"Oooh! Rabbit!"

He sped off in another completely random direction.

"Oscar?" pleaded Molly. "Forget the bunny rabbit. We need to hike to the mountain that looks like a hooked nose!"

"It'll still be there tomorrow. Mountains never move. But rabbits move fast! Very, very fast. This is excellent training for me. Coach will be so proud!"

"Please, Oscar! That mountain's five or ten miles away. We need to start walking to it immediately. We need to go back to the park. We need to find our families."

"Okay, okay," panted Oscar. "Rabbit's gone. No more distractions. Here I come."

Molly watched Oscar trot back to the hilltop.

"Sorry about that," said the dogg. "Instinct is a powerful thing, especially for athletic individuals such as myself. It kicks in, and *boom!*—It's like you're not in control of you anymore."

"If you say so," said Molly. "As an actress, I am much more in control of my emotions as well as my reactions."

That's when a butterfly flitted out of a patch of wildflowers.

Molly's tail sprang up. Her eyes bugged out.

"Butterfly!" she shouted.

"Whoa!" shouted Oscar. "Come back here! We're on a hike, remember?"

Molly ignored him and chased after the fluttering black and orange wings. She followed them into the forest and up a tree. Digging her claws into the bark she laddered up the towering evergreen effortlessly.

But then the butterfly drifted off into the open sky.

And Molly was stuck high up in the tree.

Katts are very good at climbing up trees. Climbing down from this height? Not so much.

Chapter 21

The ferret reporter scurried back to her news network's broadcasting center.

She knew this missing dogg and katt story was bigger than it seemed. Or that it *could* be bigger.

She barged into her boss's office.

"Chief!" she said. "Get ready to whip out your checkbook because you're going to double my salary after you hear my pitch."

"Go on," said the news director, a weasel, as he slumped back in his big chair, making a thoughtful steeple out of his front paws underneath his nose. The ferret paced back and forth, painting the scene for her dramatic story.

"We open on darkness!" said the ferret. "The cold shivering darkness of night."

"You mean a black screen?"

"Exactly."

"Love it," said the weasel. "Black screens are easy to shoot. And cheap, too. Go on."

"We fade in on a cute puppy, lost in the woods. Cross-dissolve to a terrified kitten, shivering in a tree, barely able to meow. Poor little creatures. They're both lost in the wilderness on the far edge of civilization."

"Puppies. Kittens. Good eye candy. Nice."

"Oh, sure—they're cuddly and fluffy and sweet," said the reporter. "On their own. Fenced off from each other. But put them together on the far edges of civilization with nothing to eat but berries and twigs and you've got nonstop action, adventure, and, most importantly, sir, CONFLICT! Remember, chief: That puppy, deep down he's a dogg. And that kitten? She's a purebred katt. Together, they are…" She framed the air with her paws. "*Lost Together: Sworn Enemies for Life!*"

"Is that the title of your piece?"

"You like it?"

"Like it? I love it!"

"Then, sir, that's the title. It's like that show we did last summer. About the polar bears and walruses stranded in the refrigerator of a fast food restaurant."

The weasel nodded. "'Survivor: Sworn Enemies.' Highest ratings we ever saw. Especially when that one walrus with the big tusks and blubbery belly got voted out of the deep freeze..."

"But this show isn't staged, boss," said the ferret. "This is *real* reality TV. A young dogg and a young katt, separated from their loved ones, lost in the wilderness, fighting against the elements while they fight against each other. Everybody knows that katts and doggs have been enemies since the beginning of time. Who can forget the Katt and Dogg War of 1812? Will these two foes find each other before the rescuers find them? If so, will the fur fly? Add in: the worried parents, banished from the search; the troubled teenage brother and sister, jealous that their siblings are the center of attention; the befuddled park rangers; the frustrated rescuers. Sir, we're talking ratings that'll go through the roof faster than a startled giraffe in a pup tent."

"What do you need to make it happen?" asked the weasel, springing out of his chair with his tail.

"Not much, sir. Just a hoot owl, some night vision goggles, a camera and..."

"And what?"

The ferret grinned. "That pay raise we were talking about, sir."

"Done and done!"

Chapter 22

Oscar perked up his ears.

Somewhere in the forest, a scaredy katt was yowling. Somewhere way up high.

He sniffed the wind.

Oh, yeah, he thought. *That's Molly.* He'd been smelling her all day. Her scent was permanently captured on his brain's internal memory chips.

Her yowls didn't sound so good. Oscar trotted along, underneath the trees, following her scent.

He came to the trunk of a tall pine and snorted along the bark.

This was the one. This was Molly's tree.

He tilted his head and looked up and up and up until he saw a lumpy shadow curled in a ball on one of the branches fifty feet above the forest floor.

"Molly?" he called out. "Is that you? It smells like you…"

"Yes, Oscar," came a faint reply. "It's me. I'm up a tree. Go ahead. Laugh."

"Okay. Ha, ha, ha." He paused. "Um, Molly?"

"What?" she shouted.

"What, exactly, am I laughing about?"

"Me! I'm stuck up a tree. Typical katt, right?"

"Yeah. It's because of your claws."

"What?"

"Katts can't climb down trees headfirst because all the claws in your paws point toward your tail."

"Is that so?"

"Yeah. I told you: I'm working on my kattology merit badge. I know all sorts of katt stuff. For instance, katts walk like camels and giraffes: You move both of your right feet first, then you move both of your left feet."

"So, tell me something, brainiac: how do we

katts climb *out* of a tree?"

"Very, very carefully," joked Oscar.

"Oscar?" Molly was sounding a little hissy. "You're not being very helpful."

"Sorry," said Oscar. "But climbing down is actually simple. Since your claws don't point the right way for a forward descent, all you have to do is *back* down the tree. At least that's what it said in the Dogg Scout Manual."

"You want me to back down the tree? Tail first?"

"Yup. Unless you want to stay up there and admire the view a little longer."

"No, thank you!"

"Then stick it in reverse!"

Oscar watched as Molly attempted to make her way, backward, down the tree.

Molly scuttled down ten feet, then stopped for a hiss break.

"Come on, katt!" urged Oscar. "You can do it!"

Molly inched down another two feet. A pair of birds on one of the branches was chirping at her.

"They're mocking me!" said Molly.

"They're mockingbirds," said Oscar. "It's what

they do. Plus, once upon a time, somebody in your family probably ate one of their cousins. Come on. Quit having a hissy fit. Keep backing up."

Molly made it another five feet down the trunk.

"I can't do this!" she said, clinging onto the bark. "I tried, but I can't!"

"Fine," said Oscar. "Jump!"

"Jump?"

"It's only twenty more feet."

"Twenty feet?"

"Don't worry. I'll catch you."

"Promise?"

Oscar crossed his webbed toes behind his back. "Promise."

"All right. Here I come!"

Molly leapt from her perch.

Oscar backed away from the tree.

Molly shrieked, spun around, shot out her legs, and crash-landed on all fours.

"That was awesome!" shouted Oscar, who found the frazzled look on Molly's frightened face to be funnier than anything he'd ever seen. "And hilarious!"

"Hilarious?" screeched Molly, narrowing her blue eyes. "I, for one, was not amused!"

"Oh, I knew you'd be okay," said Oscar. "You katts can spread out your legs like a parachute and land safely, even from way up high. For your information, there are katts who've survived falls from more than five hundred feet."

"And, for *your* information," hissed the katt, "there are many more who have suffered broken legs and worse falling out of a window or off a ladder!"

Oscar was dumbfounded. "Really?"

"Really!"

"Well, uh, they didn't mention that last bit in the Dogg Scout Manual..."

"Of course they didn't. A dogg wrote it! A dumb, ignorant, katt-hating dogg—just like you!"

Chapter 23

Molly was miffed.

Just because a few katts can sometimes fall successfully from high places doesn't mean any of them *like* doing it.

Also, katts have eyes built for hunting. They give up a little in depth perception so they can concentrate on motion detection. You need depth perception when you're falling.

"Are you okay?" the dogg asked, sheepishly.

Molly didn't answer. She wasn't hurt. But her pride sure was.

She pointed dramatically (which, as a future actress, is how she did almost everything) at the mountain peak in the distance.

"You're right," said the dogg, wagging his tail, forgetting all about the horrible trick he'd just played on Molly. "We should hike to the mountain. It's a great day for a hike or a nature walk, which is basically the same thing as a hike, wouldn't you agree?"

Molly ignored Oscar and started walking. Fast. The dogg trotted after her.

"Oh, I see. You're not speaking to me. That's okay. I'm not speaking to you, either. I mean, why should I? You're a katt, I'm a dogg. We have nothing in common so what do we have to talk about? Bones? Nope. You'd rather scratch up furniture. Rawhide chews? Forget about it. You'd rather wrestle a toy stuffed with kattnip. Hey, what is kattnip, anyhow? Is there katt in it? If so, that's kind of weird, don't you think? A katt treat made out of katts..."

Molly picked up her pace. For someone not speaking to her, the dogg sure did like to yap. He was probably part lapdogg. Molly's father told her that teeny-tiny lapdoggs yip and yap all the time. And then they put bows in their hair. Ridiculous creatures!

"It's okay we're not speaking to each other," said the dogg. "I like the sounds of silence. Especially out here in nature. I can hear a stream streaming. And crickets chirping. And the wind whipping through the treetops. It's like a whistle. A dogg whistle. That means I can hear it but you can't."

Enough, thought Molly. She spun around.

"All I can hear is *you!*" she hissed.

"Ooooh! Hello, Molly. Does this mean you're speaking to me again?"

"No."

"But you are. You're speaking to me right now."

"No. I am not."

"Yes, you are! You just did!"

Molly was about to say something but she realized that would give the dogg something to say.

So, she simply turned on her heel and hurried down the darkening trail.

"I'm glad we had that little chat," said the dogg. "Now we can just listen to the birds chirp. Although, to be honest, they might be chirping about *you*. I don't think birds like katts. I think birds hate katts even more than doggs do. I mean, at least katts don't eat doggs. Birds? Woof! You guys always have feathers sticking out of your mouths..."

Molly's ears shot up.

And not because of anything Oscar said.

She heard a low rumbling growl, off in the underbrush to her right.

She whipped around and saw it.

It was lying on a fallen tree trunk, smiling and drooling and rubbing its front paws together.

"My, my, my. A katt and a dogg. My favorite combination platter."

It was the mountain lion!

Chapter 24

*U*h-oh, thought Oscar. *The mountain lion is back! Because, duh, we're hiking toward a mountain!*

That was dumb, dumb, dumb!

Why did Oscar tell the katt to head to the mountain? Mountain lions live in mountains, otherwise they'd be called valley lions or stream lions or...

"Decisions, decisions," purred the wild mountain lion. "Which one to eat first? My cousin, the mangy katt? Or the delectable and delicious dogg?"

"I'm not mangy!" Molly hissed. "I just need time to give myself a bath."

"Mr. Mountain Lion…isn't it t-too late for b-b-breakfast?" stammered Oscar, as he gave the predator his best puppy eyes. It was a look that always worked on his mother. Puppy eyes could melt the hardest heart. He added a soft little whimper to amp up the effect.

"My, my, my. I love it when my food is cute. Such an adorable presentation."

The mountain lion padded forward.

Leaves and twigs crunched and snapped.

Oscar did not like those sounds.

Then he heard a buzzing. Probably all the terrified nerves zizzing inside his head.

"Bee!" shouted the katt. "Follow me!"

The katt bolted off after the zig-zagging bee. Oscar took off after her.

The mountain lion roared. "Come back here! Breakfast is the most important meal of the day!"

The earth shook. Oscar knew that meant the mountain lion was in hot pursuit. He picked up his pace. Forget twenty-seven miles per hour. He gunned it. He was doing thirty. Maybe thirty-five. Coach would be super proud of his wind sprint ability—if he lived long enough to tell Coach about it.

Oscar caught up with the katt. "Hop on my back!"

"What? Why? I'm a faster runner than you, dogg!"

"True. But only in sprints. Not endurance. I can maintain my speed for a long distance better than you can."

"No, thanks," said the katt, breathing heavily. "I'm better off on my own."

The mountain lion roared.

It startled the katt so much she sprang up, shot out four legs, and landed on Oscar's back.

"Yowzers! Easy with the claws!"

"Sorry," said the katt. "My bad. Head right!"

"What?"

"Dash down the hill. Into the valley. Follow that bee!"

"Why?"

"It's our best hope."

"For what?"

"Honey!"

Great, thought Oscar. *The krazy katt on my back wants to make sure her cousin, the maniac mountain lion, has honey to drizzle over his dogg meat. Sweet.*

Oscar's ears perked up. He tried to block out the snarls of the mountain lion and focus on the buzz of the bee.

Oscar isolated the sound of the lone buzzing bee. He let it lead him down a sloping hill and across a rippling stream.

Now he heard more buzzing. And more. The whole forest was humming with a swarm of buzzes.

"Yipes!" he yelped. "More bees! Dozens of them!"

"Exactly what I was hoping for!" said the katt on his back. "Follow them!"

"Where are they taking us?" Oscar wondered through his heavy panting. He was a very good long-distance runner. Usually, he didn't get winded like this. Then again, usually, he didn't have a katt riding on his back.

"They'll lead us to their hive!" said the katt. "And, if we're super lucky, we might find what we need."

"Really? What's that?"

"Another predator!"

What? thought Oscar. *Why do we need another one of those?*

He was about to find out.

Chapter 25

Molly had guessed correctly.

There was a giant grizzly bear at the beehive, enjoying his main meal of the day: a honey-coated honeycomb dripping with honey.

"Swerve left!" Molly shouted. "We need to hide behind that stump. The fur is about to fly!"

"Ours?" yelped the dogg.

"Nope," said Molly as she leapt off his back. "But that mountain lion is about to meet its match—his sworn enemy!"

Molly and Oscar ducked down.

The mountain lion raced into the clearing.

The bear roared.

The mountain lion slammed on its brakes and growled defensively.

"You're a bear," it snarled.

"Are you talking to me?" said the bear. "Are *you* talking to *me*?"

"So, sorry," said the mountain lion, sounding way too civilized for a wild beast. "Forgive the intrusion."

"Are you still talking to me?" The bear tossed its beehive aside. It stood up on its hind legs and, towering over the mountain lion, licked the honey dribbling off its claws.

"Um, very nice meeting you, bear," said the mountain lion. "Must skedaddle."

He took off running.

"Oh, you can run," the bear thundered, "but you cannot hide!"

Molly and Oscar gave the two wild creatures time to chase each other out of the valley. When they were both sure the two ferocious beasts were gone, they came out of their hiding spot behind the stump.

"You are one clever katt!" said Oscar. "You knew that bee was heading to its hive and there would be a bear there, too!"

Molly shrugged. "I had a hunch."

The dogg wagged his tail.

"You're happy, right?"

"How'd you guess?"

"Never mind. We need to keep moving."

"Okay."

"And dogg?"

"Yeah?"

"Thanks for the ride on your back. You were correct. We katts are not made for long-distance running."

"But you're excellent at being sneaky. Also pouncing."

"True. And you're very good in a marathon."

"But you also knew that bears don't like mountain lions. I didn't know that."

"Stick with me, Oscar," said Molly. "I know stuff. Especially about sworn enemies."

"You mean like us?"

"Precisely."

The dogg tilted his head sideways. "You ever wonder why that is?"

"Why what is?"

"Why do katts hate doggs?"

Molly shrugged. "I guess for the same reason doggs hate katts."

Now Oscar shrugged. "We just do, I guess. We

always have and we probably always will. More of that instinct stuff."

Molly nodded. "It's just the way of the world. Come on. We need to keep moving. That mountain isn't going to walk to us."

"Nope," said Oscar. "You want to ride on my back again?"

"No, that's okay."

"I insist," said Oscar. "And this time, could you give me a good scratch behind the ears? Maybe a little shoulder rub?"

"No, Oscar. I am not going to be your personal masseuse!"

"Come on! I can't reach those spots."

"No. Not going to happen."

"Pretty please? With tuna on top?"

"Nope."

Happily bickering, Molly and Oscar headed off, hoping they'd reach the mountain shaped like a hooked nose before sunset.

Or before they bumped into another wild predator more interested in katts and doggs than honey or mountain lions.

Chapter 26

Oscar's family was back home in Doggsylvania, huddled around their television set, watching the gripping news story on TV.

"The dogg's name is Oscar," the ferret reporter said to the camera. "He has been missing now for two days. Lost in the woods. Battling the elements. Frightened by every sound he hears, every shadow he sees. His tail, no doubt, permanently tucked between his legs."

The screen filled with Oscar's most recent class picture, the one where his eyes were closed and his tongue was hanging out of his mouth.

"That's my boy!" said his father, Duke.

"Oh, Duke!" whined his mother. "Will we ever see that sweet, sweet smile again?"

"Sure, we will, Lola," said Duke. "We'll get the picture back. I just loaned it to the ferret so she could show it on TV."

"That's not what I meant, Duke!" blubbered Oscar's mother. "What if Oscar never comes home?"

"Aw, don't give yourself kennel cough, Lola! That freaky hawkowl promised us she'd find our boy. Plus, they have those crocodile-lions and grizzly wolves."

"Can I have his toys?" said Fifi.

"What?"

"While Oscar is missing or lost or whatever, can I have his toys? Most of his still have their squeakers."

When Fifi said that, Oscar's mother howled so loudly, all the neighbors heard it and immediately joined in.

"Now look what you've done, Fifi," said Duke. "You made your mother so sad, she started a howl fest. This could go on all night."

Fifi rolled her eyes. "They usually do. May I please be excused? I want to go curl up in a ball and take a nap."

"But they're talking about your brother on TV," sniffled her mom.

"I know. That's why I need to take a nap. Borrr-ring."

"You stay right here young lady and...*grrrrrrrr!*"

Duke's attention snapped back to the TV screen. So did Fifi and Lola's. Now the ferret was interviewing that snooty katt family, the one with the missing daughter.

"I'm here with Boomer Hissleton the Third, Esquire," said the reporter. "You're the father of the missing katt, Molly, is that correct?"

"Indeed."

"How do you feel about your daughter being lost in the woods with her sworn enemy, a dogg?"

"How do you think I feel? Horrible. Ghastly. Sickened. Oh, the horror! Lost in the forest while a fiendish mutt is on the prowl. It's unimaginably horrific!"

"That snobby katt makes me want to chase my tail until I catch it!" said Duke.

"I hope Oscar chases that stupid katt up a tree," said Fifi.

"I agree," said Lola. "It's the katt's fault that our Oscar is missing."

"Um, how's that work, Mom?" asked Fifi.

"Simple. The katt did it first. She was missing before Oscar."

Duke arched an eyebrow. "Lola?" he snarled. "Did you just call our son a copykatt?"

"Oh, dear. I did, didn't I? I'm so, so sorry." She tilted back her head and howled.

And once again, the whole neighborhood joined in.

Chapter 27

It was after dark, which meant that Molly was wide awake.

Katts are nocturnal creatures. They do their best work after the sun has set. That's why the katts' shops and grocery stores stay open till six a.m. Most bargain-hunting and food-gathering in Kattsburgh takes place well after midnight.

Oscar the dogg, on the other hand, was starting to yawn.

"Maybe we should think about setting up camp for the night," he said.

"Let's keep going," said Molly.

"But we can't even see the mountain anymore."

"Sure we can. It's that dark lump next to that darker lump under the twinkling star."

"Which twinkling star?" said Oscar, sounding exasperated. "There's a billion of 'em!"

"Look, dogg," said Molly. "I'm a katt. I do my best work at night."

"Night is when you're supposed to sleep!" said Oscar.

"Only if you're a dogg!"

"Which I am!"

"Tell me something I couldn't already smell!"

While they argued they came to a road lined with cornstalks. As they squabbled, their voices grew louder and louder. Before long, they were barking and caterwauling at each other.

Big mistake.

"Get off my land!" shouted a cranky voice in the darkness. "This is my farm, you varmints!"

"We're not on your farm!" shouted Oscar. "We're just lost!"

"Git!"

"Look," said Molly, "it's like Oscar said: We're not on your farm. We're on a road."

"It's *my* road!" answered the voice. "And this here…"

Molly heard something go click.

"This is my shotgun. I ain't afraid to use it, neither! Now vamoose!"

"I'm not a moose!" hollered Oscar. "I'm a dogg."

"And I'm a katt," added Molly.

"We're lost!" they shouted together.

"And hungry," said Oscar.

"And cold," said Molly.

"And we were chased by a mountain lion this morning," said Oscar. "And then we hiked like twenty miles…"

"Frankly," sighed Molly, "we're miserable."

"And scared," whispered Oscar.

They heard footsteps. A row of cornstalks swayed open like a curtain to reveal one of the strangest creatures Molly had ever seen.

She was a doggkatt!

Chapter 28

Oscar couldn't stop gawping at the doggkatt. His mouth hung open. Stringy drool dribbled out.

"What you gawkin' at, young'un?" said the doggkatt, sounding like somebody's grumpy grandmother who doesn't like it when you pee on her sofa.

"Sorry," said Oscar. "Didn't mean to be rude. It's just that I've never seen a creature that was half katt and half dogg."

"Me, neither," added Molly. "Not even in a monster movie."

The granny grinned. "We are rare indeed. Even here in this magical park. Reckon there's only a half dozen of us left."

Oscar and Molly just nodded. They didn't want the old doggkatt to know how much she was creeping them out.

"You say you're lost?"

Oscar and Molly nodded some more. They also tried to smile.

"And hungry?"

They nodded one more time. They did not, however, move any closer to the weird creature from the cornfield. She walked on her two legs but she wasn't wearing clothes, which meant she was wild. But usually "wild" meant "really mean and hoping to eat you" like the mountain lion. Why was she being so nice?

"Well, come along then," she said. "You two can spend the night in my cabin. I'll fix you something to eat."

Eat? Oscar gulped. *What if the freaky freak was also part mountain lion?*

"Don't worry, dogg," the old creature laughed, as if she could read Oscar's mind. "I ain't gonna eat you or your katt friend. How could I? Why, you two remind me of my great-great-grandparents."

"Um, we're not really friends," mumbled Oscar.

"We just called a temporary truce," added Molly. "Friendship's not really in the cards for us."

"We're sworn enemies," said Oscar.

"More's the shame," sighed the elderly dogg-katt. "I wish I could get you home myself, but these bones are too old for the journey. Just keep your noses pointed to Crooked Nose Mountain. Come on, shake a tailfeather. I've got supper on the stove. I like to eat late at night. Reckon it's the katt in me..."

She led them down the road to her cabin. Oscar could smell the odors of something foul wafting on the breeze.

"I didn't know wild animals lived in houses," Molly said.

"I reckon there's a lot you 'civilized' folk don't

know about us 'wild' ones," said the doggkatt. "Here now, I fixed up a fish stew."

Oscar whimpered.

"Don't worry," said the doggkatt. "It's kattfish."

Oscar wagged his tail. Slightly. Kattfish might be okay. Especially if you're starving.

They sat down to supper and buried their faces in their bowls.

Oscar loved the stew.

"This fish is delish!" he said, his tail thumping against a leg of his stool.

"An old family recipe," said the granny. "So, what are your names?"

"I'm Oscar!"

"Molly."

"You two can call me Granny," said the wrinkled doggkatt. "Most everybody in these parts does."

"So, uh, how'd you, you know, become...you?" asked Oscar.

"Well, according to my parents—who heard the story from their parents—my great-great-grandfather and great-great-grandmother were a dogg and a katt, just like you two. They got lost in the wilderness, just like you two. They had a lot of close scrapes and angry words but, eventually, they realized that the only way the two of them could survive out here on the far edge of civilization was to work together."

"Just like the hawkowl," said Molly.

"Who?" said Granny.

"She's the head ranger down at the Western Frontier Park," explained Oscar. "She's weird, too. Just like you."

Granny smiled. "I like you, Oscar. You say what's on your mind without giving it a second thought."

"He's a dogg," said Molly. "They're not big on thoughts—first or second ones."

"If you ask me," said Oscar, "you combo critters are super cool. Hawkowls. Doggkatts. I bet you can run great distances *and* be sneaky at the same time!"

Granny chuckled. "Yes, I could. When I was younger, anyways…"

"It's like you have superpowers just like super heroes in comic books!"

The wise old doggkatt shook her head. "Not all of us, Oscar. Some 'combo critters'—as you call them—some are super evil super villains."

Oscar gulped again. "Which ones?"

"Beware of the weaselboars."

Chapter 29

Molly was hanging on to the wise old woman's every word.

"The weaselboars, as you might've reckoned," she said, "are half weasel and half boar."

"They're boring?" asked Oscar.

"A boar," explained Molly, "is a wild pig with curling tusks! Very ferocious."

"And these weaselboars?" said Granny. "Even though they're combo critters, they stayed wild. They're the most dangerous beasts in the park. You know, living out here in the woods like I do,

I'm a big fan of animals getting along, helping each other. Becoming something more together than they could apart. Your hawkowl. Your moose-horse. In most cases, they're better together. But the weaselboar? They're worse."

"How come?" asked Oscar.

"What do you children know about weasels?"

"They run a very popular TV network," said Molly.

"That's in your civilized world," said Granny. "Out here? Weasels are nonstop killing machines. They're cunning predators who'll hunt all day and all night. They can climb, swim, and run. And since their bodies are so long and skinny, they can raid underground burrows, follow rodents into small hidey-holes, or wrap themselves around larger prey to hold 'em still while they bite. Weasels kill more than they can eat. They hang on to the extra, storing it like leftovers, just in case they get hungry for a between-meal snack."

Now Molly gulped the way Oscar had been gulping.

"And the wild boars?" Granny clucked her

tongue. "They're mean, nasty, and big. The king of pests. When they attack, they don't stop until their target is plum dead. Put the two together and what've you got?"

"A nightmare!" said Molly.

Granny nodded. "Also available in broad daylight."

Molly and Oscar pushed away their fish stew bowls. Neither one of them was in the mood for seconds.

"I reckon you two must be exhausted," said Granny, creaking up from the table. "You can bunk down up in the loft. I'll pack you some food in the mornin' and you can be on your merry way. Sweet dreams."

Yeah, right, thought Molly. *As if that would even be possible with visions of weaselboars dancing in our heads.*

But the ancient doggkatt was correct. Molly and Oscar were pooped. Warm food in their bellies had made them both even drowsier. They climbed up a ladder into the sleeping loft.

"Tomorrow," said Oscar, "I'll help you climb

back down. And this time, I promise I'll catch you. Or you can ride down on my back."

"Thanks, Oscar. I appreciate that. Good night."

"Good night, Molly. Sleep tight. Don't let the weaselboars bite!"

Chapter 30

Oscar was awake at dawn.

Molly slept for five extra hours.

Typical katt. But Oscar waited for her. And then he helped her climb backward down the ladder.

"You can do it," he coached. "Just put one paw behind the other."

After Molly very slowly climbed down three rungs, she jumped. This time, Oscar caught her.

Granny fed them both a hearty breakfast of kibble mush. While they gobbled it down, she put packets of food and biscuits into a bright red bandana lying flat on the kitchen table. "You're still a long way away from Crooked Nose Mountain. Are you two sure you don't want to stay here where it's safe a little spell longer?"

"Thank you for the offer, Granny," said Oscar, "but I miss my family. When doggs worry, we whimper. I don't want my mother to whimper."

"When katts worry, they lose fur," said Molly. "I don't want my mother to go bald."

"Very well, then," said Granny, tying the bandana up into a bundle and knotting it onto a long broom handle. "Be safe, and always remember: no matter what your math teacher may say, one plus one sometimes equals more than two. We're always stronger when we work together."

Granny took Oscar and Molly's paws into hers, bowed her head, and prayed.

Oscar prayed, too. Mostly he prayed that all the weaselboars had taken the week off.

Refreshed, with their stomachs full, Oscar and Molly thanked Granny and set off for Crooked Nose Mountain, and hopefully, the Western Frontier Park, where they would be reunited with their families.

About an hour after they'd left Granny's farm and were, once again, deep in the forest—swatting gnats and flies and mosquitos with their tails—Oscar had a thought.

"Hey, Molly?"

"Yeah, Oscar?"

"Do you think that, if we worked together, we might turn into some kind of incredibly awesome creature with superpowers?"

"Maybe. But I don't want a dogg head. I need my blue eyes for all the movies I'm going to act in."

"Yeah, and I wouldn't want a katt butt. It'd smell funny."

They kept hiking in silence—each one thinking about what the wise old doggkatt had said about sticking together.

But that silence was soon interrupted by the roar of raging rapids.

There was a fast river between them and the mountain.

"We need to turn back!" cried Molly, because katts are terrified of water.

"But the park is near the mountain."

"I can't swim!" said Molly.

"I can," said Oscar. "I can doggy paddle."

"Oh, great. You're going to abandon me?"

"I didn't say that." He handed her the pole with the food bundle. "You carry this. I'll carry you."

"What?"

"You can climb on my back again and I'll swim us both safely to the other side."

Molly grinned. "Still trying to get your back scratched, huh?"

Oscar laughed. "Yeah. And behind my ears, too. Come on, katt. We need to swim together or we'll probably drown alone."

Molly clambered up on Oscar's back.

Oscar waded into the rippling stream.

"Ready?" he said.

"Yeah. But try not to splash too much!"

They both took a long deep breath.

The current was swift. Oscar had to paddle extra hard to avoid being washed downstream with all the tree branches rushing by, swept along by whitewater rapids.

Finally, with Oscar fighting the fatigue in his leg muscles, they made it to the far shore. Oscar lumbered up the slippery rocks to safety. Then, panting hard, he collapsed in an exhausted heap.

"Look what I grabbed us for supper!" said Molly. "Another kattfish!"

"Yum," said Oscar, standing up and shaking his body to dry off. He accidentally spritzed Molly with a shower of sprinkles. "Oops, sorry! My bad."

"Ah, that's okay. We made it across the river."

"And you caught us fresh fish for dinner! We *are* better together. Oh, yes we are!"

They both laughed and high-fived each other's paws in triumph.

They were so happy, so caught up in their new team's first victory, they didn't see the creature slinking through the trees toward them.

Chapter 31

"I'll gather some wood to make a cooking fire!" said Oscar. "Doggs are great at hauling branches and twigs. I have a friend, he's a Labrador, and he drags half a tree around with him wherever he goes."

"I have friends who do the same thing with mice," said Molly. "You build the fire, I'll clean the kattfish. Together, we'll feast!"

Oscar wagged his tail. "We make an awesome team, don't we, katt?"

"We have our moments," said Molly.

Oscar scampered off to the nearest tree. He was nosing around, looking for the perfect pieces of wood for his campfire when he smelled something absolutely disgusting. Like poop mixed with wet fur mixed with rancid oil.

His ears stood up when he heard a low, throaty rumble. The hackles on his back shot out. He backed two paces away from the tree.

"What's wrong?" asked Molly.

"I'm not sure," said Oscar. "But I've never smelled *anything* so foul, disgusting, revolting, or gross."

"Well, that's not a very polite thing to say," said a deep, grumbling voice.

Something stepped out of the thick underbrush near the tree.

A weaselboar!

"Gathering firewood?" it asked. Gristly slobber hung off its tusks like double strands of snot. "Were you two getting ready to eat?"

Oscar backed up quickly and huddled with Molly.

"Speaking of eating things," wheezed a second

weaselboar as it slipped out of the shrubbery. "What's for dinner tonight?"

"I think it's those two," said a third.

"With an appetizer of kattfish," said a fourth, popping out of the shadows on their right. "And whatever's tied up in that red bandana."

Molly and Oscar were completely surrounded.

"What's in the food bundle?" asked the first weaselboar, licking its slimy tusks with a slippery tongue.

"Nothing," said Oscar, trying his best to protect the food Granny had given them for their trek.

"It's food!" said Molly. "Delicious, homemade food. You can have it."

"Psst," whispered Oscar out of the side of his snout. "We need that, Molly. For our hike up the mountain."

"We also need to be alive!" Molly whispered back.

"True," said Oscar. "Good point." Oscar turned to the leader of the weaselboar pack. "Enjoy, fellas. Our food is your food."

"We know," said the leader of the pack.

All four snarling beasts pounced on the fish and plump bandana.

When they were finished, there was nothing left but a few tattered shreds of checkered red cloth and a couple snapped-in-half fish bones.

The weaselboars belched.

"Not bad for fish," said the leader. "But we prefer red meat. The kind you find inside katts and doggs!"

Chapter 32

Oscar looked at Molly.

Molly looked at Oscar.

"Run!" they both shouted.

They took off like a double bolt of terrified lightning.

Oscar saw Molly zigzagging to the left. He sprinted to the right, bobbing and weaving, juking and jiving. His coach would've been proud.

The weaselboars formed a pack and took off after Molly.

They undoubtedly knew she couldn't run as

fast as Oscar over long distances. But, since they weren't chasing after Oscar, he could escape. He had a clear path to freedom!

Molly would probably die but Oscar would definitely live.

Wow, thought Oscar as he bounded away. *Who'd ever of thought that a katt would die for* me?

Of course, it wasn't exactly a *choice* Molly was making, but still, it was very noble of her.

Then Oscar thought about how she'd caught them a kattfish.

And how she'd scratched behind his ears while they crossed the raging rapids.

And how she didn't mind when he shook off all that water and splashed her even though katts hate water.

Finally he remembered what the wise old doggkatt had told them. *Sometimes one plus one equals more than two.*

Oscar had to admit...he and Molly made a great team. Even though she was a katt.

"Two can play at this game!" he said aloud. "I can be noble, too!"

He slammed on the brakes, did a one-eighty around a tree, and ran after the four weaselboars who were chasing after Molly like a sixteen-legged bulldozer.

"Out of my way, fatsos!" he shouted. Then he sprang up and over the quivering wall of stinky weaselboar butts because he was part springer spaniel on his father's side.

He landed six inches in front of a tusk and kicked his motor into high gear.

He could see Molly up ahead. She was still zigging and zagging but she was also slowing down and breathing hard.

Good at sprints, thought Oscar. *Long distances? Not so much.*

He dug down deep, found a little extra oomph, and picked up his pace.

In a flash, he was running alongside Molly.

"Hop on!" he shouted.

This time, she didn't hesitate. She leapt onto his back.

"Thanks," she gasped as she clasped his collar with her claws.

"I think I can outrun those four bozos," said Oscar. "They're fast, but they're also kind of fat and out of shape. I'll just lead them on a merry—"

Oscar didn't get to finish that thought.

Because, all of a sudden, he and Molly caught in a tangle of ropes that was whooshing them up...up...up into the crown of a leafy tree.

"It's a trap!" said Molly.

"But they're wild animals!" whined Oscar as he and Molly bobbed up and down. "How'd they weave a net?"

"We studied with some very clever spiders," said the leader of the weaselboars, looking up at the trapped katt and dogg while licking its chops.

"It's one of our special skills," said the nastiest looking weaselboar in the bunch. "We use our tusks like knitting needles."

Combo critters, thought Oscar, remembering what Granny had told them about the hybrid creatures with the amazing abilities. *Some are super evil super villains.*

And some were about to eat Oscar and Molly for din-din.

Chapter 33

Molly was expecting the dirty and disgusting weaselboars to gobble them down right away.

But they didn't.

"It's not every day that we trap meat as sweet and tender as you two," said the leader as the beasts dragged the net back to their den. "The king will wish to join us for this particular feast."

The other weaselboars snorted in agreement.

Molly was doing her best to act like she wasn't afraid. She was channeling every heroine from every movie she'd ever seen. She shot the weasel-boars a bold and angry look of defiance. Of course, she was being dragged along a bumpy trail on her butt so she wasn't sure she was totally selling the whole "you don't scare me" thing.

"Put them in the den!" shouted the leader of the pack when they came to a muddy clearing under some twisted and knotty trees. Two weaselboars slashed open the rope net with their tusks. Two others nudged Molly and Oscar into a burrow beneath the shallow roots of a tree.

"It's nice and cool down in the hole," chortled the leader. "Just like a refrigerator. It'll keep you chilled and fresh until the king arrives."

Molly and Oscar tumbled underground into the cold and damp hole. The weaselboars shoved a boulder across the entrance of the den to seal off the only exit.

Molly and Oscar were trapped. In the dark.

"I guess we're prisoners now," said Oscar.

"No," said Molly. "I think we're still dinner."

"I'm sorry I ran right into their trap," said Oscar.

"You ran back to rescue me," said Molly. "It was like something a brother would do. If, you know, my brother wasn't so easily distracted by bright, shiny objects. So, do you have any sibs?"

"Just one. A sister. Her name is Fifi. She's kind of a pampered pooch. I wonder if she even misses me. She probably already stole all the toys out of my room…"

"My brother, Blade, has the attention span of a flea," said Molly. "His favorite hobby is to chase reflections on the wall. Or the floor. Sometimes, I drive him crazy with my fanciest collar."

"How?"

"It has rhinestones on it. So, I sit in the sun and bounce little light sparkles all over the place. He can never decide which one to chase first. Drives him bananas."

"I like to bury my sister's hair bows in the back-yard. That makes her nutso."

Molly sighed.

Then Oscar sighed.

"I miss Blade," said Molly.

"Yeah," said Oscar. "I miss Fifi, too."

"Too bad we'll never see them again."

The dogg sprang up, fully alert. Even in the darkness of the den, Molly could see a determined glint in his eyes.

"Unless…" he said.

"Unless what?"

"Thinking about burying my sister's hair bows reminded me of something."

"What?"

Oscar wagged his tail, proudly. "Not to brag, but I'm a very, very, *very* good digger!"

Chapter 34

Oscar sniffed the walls of the underground den.

"Dirt," he muttered.

He moved his nose to the left. Took in a deep snort through his nostrils.

"More dirt."

He shifted his nose thirty degrees to the right. "Dirt." Forty degrees. "Dirt."

He sniffed harder.

"And...weeds! More specifically, dandelions. Judging by the lag time between the dirt scent and the first hint of something wet, mustardy, and green, this wall is only six inches thick! I can dig through that in a heartbeat! Stand back, katt. The mud clods are about to fly."

Oscar went to work on the clay wall. Clumps of muck and pebbles and shredded tree roots went sailing.

"*Oof,*" he heard Molly exclaim behind him when a chunk of something must've hit her. "Ouch!"

"Sorry," he said.

"Don't be sorry! Just dig us out of here. I'm too young, talented, and beautiful to be dinner for a weaselboar!"

Finally, Oscar saw a pinprick of sunlight. A few more paw loads of dirt and sunlight was streaming into the underground burrow.

"Just…need…to…make…the…hole…a…little…wider," Oscar murmured as he kept digging as hard and fast as he could.

"That hole's big enough for me to squeeze through!" said Molly.

"We both have to climb out," said Oscar.

"Then keep digging!"

Finally, Oscar scooped out a hole wide enough for him to climb out of, too. "I'll go first. If there's a guard, I'll growl and snarl at him. You climb up after me and jump on my back. We're going to need to run another marathon."

"Got it," said Molly. "And Oscar?"

"Yeah, Molly?"

"Kind of, sort of thanks."

"You're welcome. Kind of, sort of. You ready?"

"Ready!"

"On three. One, two…"

"Do we go on three or after three?"

"After three would be four."

"So, we go on three?"

"I do. You follow right after me."

"So, I'm actually going on four, correct?"

"Fine," said Oscar. "I'm not good at math. One, two…three!"

Oscar scurried out of the hole. He spun around.

There was only one weaselboar standing guard at the entrance to the den. And he was lying on the rock, taking a nap.

"Hee-yah!" shouted Molly, shooting out of the tunnel like a furry cannonball. She used Oscar's head like a gymnast would a pommel horse, did a flip, a midair sideways twist, landed on his back, and, saddled behind his shoulders, was ready to ride Oscar to freedom. "Giddyup!"

Unfortunately, all her excited shouting woke up the snoozing weaselboar.

"Hang on!" shouted Oscar. He started running through the forest.

The startled weaselboar guard quickly realized what was going on: the king's feast was escaping.

Snorting wildly, it took off after Oscar and Molly, who kept looking over her shoulder, giving a play-by-play commentary.

"The weaselboar is in hot pursuit. He stumbled over our exit hole. That's good. Uh-oh. He looks really, really mad. That's bad…"

The trees thinned out. Oscar saw a cliff up ahead. A rocky precipice. And there was nothing on the other side but sky and clouds.

Chapter 35

Molly felt the dogg slam on his brakes as they raced dangerously close to the edge of the cliff.

"We're trapped!" she cried out, dramatically. "Again."

The ground shook. She could hear the rampaging weaselboar's heavy hooves pounding into the dirt as it chased after them.

Molly climbed off the dogg's back.

"Stay behind me," said Oscar, shielding her body with his. The dumb dogg started inching backward, moving them closer to the cliff. "I want to be right on the edge."

"What? Why?"

"Just let me know when we get there. I can't turn around. I have to keep my eyes on the weaselboar."

"Oscar? Why would anybody want to stand on the edge of a cliff? It's a sheer drop."

"How far?"

Molly held her breath and dared to peek down into the ravine. "Three hundred feet. At least."

"Perfect," said the dogg. "Hang on. Here it comes."

"Are you demented? It's going to knock us off the bluff."

"No, it's not!"

Oscar crouched into a defensive stance, protecting Molly, who peeked between his legs and saw the weaselboar lower its head. With its head down and curled tusks pointed straight at Oscar, the ferocious beast charged forward.

Oscar just stood there, defending Molly.

When the beast was maybe six inches away

and Molly could smell the hot breath streaming out of its flared snout, Oscar finally leaned sharply to his right.

Molly leaned with him.

The giant weaselboar became a blur.

Molly heard something sharp slice across Oscar's fur.

But he didn't wince in pain. Instead, he wagged his tail. Because he was happily watching the weaselboar's momentum carry it over the cliff.

The thud came ten seconds later. It was a very, very long drop.

"You saved us!" shouted Molly. "Woo-hoo! You are the bravest dogg I've ever met."

"Thanks," wheezed Oscar.

Then Molly saw a bright-red gash sliced across his side. It was oozing blood. The charging weaselboar's razor-sharp tusk had slashed him!

"You're hurt!" said Molly.

"Nah. It's just a scratch."

"That thing was going to gore you! To stab you with its tusk."

"True. But I'm nimble. It missed. *Whoo...*"

Oscar stumbled slightly.

Molly pushed him away from the edge of the cliff.

"Is it hot out here or is it me?" said the dogg, sounding all sorts of woozy. "Why are all the trees spinning like that? And how come the ground feels wobbly and spongy, like it's a trampoline?"

"Take it easy," said Molly. "You're bleeding really badly."

Oscar limped forward. "I told you. It's just a

scraaa—" His knees buckled. He collapsed and toppled to the ground.

"Oscar?" said Molly. "Are you okay? Oscar?"

He didn't answer. He just lay there in the dirt, bleeding.

Molly knew what she had to do. She had to run. Fast!

Chapter 36

Oscar shivered even though he was burning up with fever.

He wished he could take off his fur coat but he was a dogg. The heavy coat was permanently attached.

He felt dizzy. If he weren't already lying on the ground, he'd probably collapse again.

There was a throbbing pain in the side of his chest—right where the weaselboar had nicked him with its tusk. The bloody line had turned into a scabby scar coated with little flakes of leaves.

Not exactly a sterile dressing but rolling over and letting Mother Nature cake the wound had actually stopped the bleeding.

"Molly?" he cried weakly. "Molly?"

The katt didn't answer.

Oscar raised his head slightly and looked around.

The katt was gone. She'd probably taken off two seconds after Oscar hit the ground.

"I saved her," he muttered. "She abandoned me. Typical katt. All they care about is themselves."

His head fell back to the ground with a heavy thud.

"Ooof!"

Now Oscar had a splitting headache to go with his throbbing chest ache and his raging fever.

And he was alone. In the wilderness. At night.

He could hear mountain lions off in the distance. Howling wolves and coyotes, too.

Flat on his back, Oscar looked up at the stars and realized: This was going to be his last night on earth. He was going to die in the middle of nowhere with nobody around.

"Good-bye, Mom," he whimpered. "I'm sorry I ran off like that. It wasn't because of your picnic food. I'm just a runner, I guess. Good-bye, Dad. I hope you never find out that I spent the last few days of my life with a katt. I know how mad that would make you. I thought she was different, you know? Turns out she was just like all the other katts. When the going got tough, she ran off and left me. Good-bye, Fifi. You can have all my toys. Try not to break all the squeakers at once."

He wheezed.

It felt like a Saint Bernard was sitting on his chest.

"You can have my stash of jerky strips, too. Look under the pillow in my dogg bed…"

He had to stop talking to himself.

Breathing was getting harder and harder. The walls of his chest felt like they were on fire.

Oscar closed his eyes and breathed a heavy sigh.

There was nothing to do now except—

He heard something approaching.

He knew he was a goner. An easy target, sprawled out in the clearing, spotlighted by the moon.

Who was sneaking up to eat him? The dead weaselboar's angry cousins or that mountain lion? Maybe it'd be somebody new, like a crazy coyote.

He worked open one weakened eye to see who his attacker was going to be. And saw a katt with white fur and brilliant blue eyes staring straight down at him.

"Molly?" he murmured.

"Shhh!" she said. "Don't talk."

"Did you miss me?"

"No, not exactly. Maybe a little..."

Oscar grinned as best he could. "Kind of, sort of thank you," he said.

"You're kind of, sort of welcome. Now be quiet and stay still. You're a mess. I have major work to do."

Chapter 37

Unfortunately, Molly did what she knew she had to do first.

She licked the dogg's totally gross wound with her sandpaper tongue.

"That tickles," giggled Oscar.

"Be still, dogg," said Molly, trying to act like a trained nurse would because her mother was a nurse (and Molly secretly hoped to play a nurse on a TV series about the emergency room in a hospital one day).

"Why are you licking me?" Oscar asked, trying

hard not to giggle again. He was very ticklish.

"Because," Molly explained, "saliva contains a tissue factor that helps promote the blood clotting mechanism."

"Really?"

"Really. My mom's a nurse. Licking a wound is our way of applying disinfectant."

"So why does your tongue feel like sandpaper?"

"It's specially equipped with tiny backward hooks that turn our tongues into excellent grooming brushes. It's why we always look so much better than you guys."

"So, why'd you run away?"

"Who says I ran away?"

"Me. You weren't here when I woke up after I passed out, which, by the way, happened right after I saved your life."

"I left because I had to go find medicinal herbs. My mother taught me all about them. For instance, honey. It's a great way to speed up wound healing. I also found some calendula, marshmallow root, and lavender."

"I like the way the lavender smells..."

"It's not for your nose, Oscar. It's for your wounds. It can also help fight against infection and reduce the pain."

Molly applied all the medicinal herbs she'd been able to track down in the forest.

"I wish I had some peppermint," she mumbled. "It can help with your aches and pains."

Oscar didn't say anything. Feeling better but still weak, he was drifting off to sleep.

"Peppermint could also help cure your dogg breath." Molly waved her paw under her nose. "It smells like a cow died in your mouth."

"Sorry," mumbled Oscar. Soon, he was snoring. Then his legs started kicking like he was chasing squirrels in his dreams.

Or maybe it was a nightmare and he was running away from weaselboars with Molly riding on his back.

"Did you know that katts have always been worshipped as gods?" she asked.

Oscar didn't answer.

"Did you know katts spend seventy percent of our day sleeping and fifteen percent grooming, which only leaves fifteen percent for everything else—like taking care of a dogg who risked his life to save mine?"

Oscar didn't say a word. He was out like a light.

Molly bent down close to his ear.

"Did you also know that you're very brave? Because you are, Oscar. You are."

Chapter 38

Meanwhile, back home in civilization, Oscar and Molly's stories were splashed all over cable TV.

The media had turned the story of the missing children into a nonstop, action-adventure tale, complete with animations of "what might be going on." Molly and Oscar were heroes in their hometowns.

Molly's picture appeared on milk and cream cartons throughout Kattsburgh.

In Doggsylvania, Oscar's photo was featured on billboards and the back of kibble bags.

The ferret reporter at the Weasel Broadcasting Network had taken her idea about the sworn enemies lost together in the wilderness and turned it into TV's top-rated tabloid TV show.

"Still no sign of Oscar and Molly," she said to her nightly audience. "If they're both still alive, one has to wonder: Have the two sworn enemies met each other out there in the unforgiving wilderness? And, if so, have they killed each other? Stay tuned!"

There was an ominous *dun-dun-dun* sound effect as the image on the screen cut to Molly's father, Boomer Hissleton the Third, Esquire, at home in his stuffy study.

"Doggs are dirty, disgusting, and dangerous," he said.

"And dumb," added his son, Blade. "They're, like, total dumbskulls."

"He means numbskulls," said the father.

"Whatever," said the son.

"We'll hear from the dogg's parents," said the ferret, "right after this word from our sponsor, Clumpy Lumpy's Kitty Litter. Remember: only doggs pee on trees."

After the commercial, the ferret was sitting with Oscar's family in their rumpus room. Squeak toys, bouncy balls, and half-chewed rawhide bones littered the floor.

"What do you think your son will do if he encounters a katt out in the wilds of the Western Frontier Park?" the ferret asked Oscar's father.

"What any self-respecting dogg would do," he told her. "Chase that filthy feline up a tree."

"My little brother is good at chasing things," added his teenage sister. "Like his tail. I once saw him chase his tail for fifteen whole minutes."

After the interview, the ferret showed footage of all the dogg neighbors dropping by the house with casserole dishes of kibble mush and heaping platters of sliced meats.

"Look at all this roast beef and corned beef and the all-beef frankfurters!" said Oscar's father, licking his chops. "Maybe my son should get lost in the wilderness more often!"

Oscar's mom slugged him in the shoulder.

"I was just making a joke, Lola!"

"This is no time for jokes, Duke."

"You're right, Lola. It's time to eat!"

"Things aren't quite as rambunctious back at the katt house," the ferret told her audience.

The scene shifted again.

The Hissleton family was sitting in a circle with a dozen other katts.

"We call it a clowder," explained Molly's mother, Fluffy. "That's a cluster of katts. It's our support group. I find it very comforting to have our friends and neighbors dropping by like this on a daily basis to practice active listening and positive enablement."

"I just wish they'd bring food," added her son, Blade.

Chapter 39

Back in the wilderness, in the thick forest ringing the base of Crooked Nose Mountain, Oscar managed to walk with the help of a crutch he'd fashioned out of a tree branch.

"You sure you want to keep on hiking?" Molly asked him.

"Yeah. No problem. I'm fine."

Maybe if Oscar hadn't winced with excruciating pain every time he said one of those words, Molly might've believed him.

"You're wounded, Oscar," said Molly. "The weaselboar really got you."

"I know. I was there when it happened, remember?"

"Maybe we should rest. I could put some more honey on your wound."

"No. We should just climb over that snow-capped mountain and head down to the Western Frontier base camp on the other side."

"You're definitely tough, dogg."

"Thank you."

"And brave."

"You, too. I used to think all katts were scaredy katts. My father says you guys are so skittish you jump at the slightest noise. You hear something—*boom!*—you screech, your fur shoots up, you go flying."

"Our fur shoots up to make us look bigger," explained Molly.

"Really?"

"It's a defense mechanism. If we look bigger, a predator might leave us alone."

"Huh. I didn't know that. I thought you katts just did that puffy fur thing because you enjoy looking like you just stuck your paw in a wall socket."

"Well," said Molly, "my father says you doggs like to scoot on your tails and drag your butts across the carpet."

"Nope. He's wrong. We only do that when we *have* to."

"And when do you have to do it?"

"About once or twice a week."

Limping along for hours, Oscar and Molly finally arrived at the foot of the funny-looking mountain. There was a rutted dirt road winding its way up to the snowy peak.

"If there's a road," said Oscar, his tail starting to wag, "there have to be some vehicles. Why else would anybody build a road except to drive on it?"

"We could hitch a ride!" exclaimed Molly. "I'll bet this road leads to the Western Frontier Park. We're going home, Oscar. Civilization, here we come!"

"Woo-hoo!"

Their luck got even better.

They heard a rumbling engine and the crunch of tires off in the distance.

"Stick out your paw, Molly, and poke up a claw!" said Oscar. "Here comes our ride!"

Molly, who was shorter than Oscar, stepped in front of him and stuck out her paw. Smiling, glad that his ordeal was almost over, Oscar stuck out his paw, too.

A trundling truck rounded a bend, stirring up a cloud of dust.

Suddenly, Molly's fur poofed straight out. She looked twice her size.

Oscar tapped her on the shoulder. "Um, why are you activating your defense mechanism, Molly?"

"Don't you see who's behind the wheel?"

Oscar narrowed his eyes and peered at the truck.

Uh-oh.

It was being driven by a weaselboar.

Chapter 40

For a second, Molly thought about pointing at Oscar and screaming, "He's the one! He's the dogg who made your cousin jump off the cliff."

But if she did, she knew the weaselboar behind the wheel of the truck would shred her to pieces ten seconds after it shredded Oscar. Besides, they were in this together now.

"Tuck and roll!" she shouted.

"Huh?"

Molly's father always said you couldn't teach

an old dogg new tricks. Seemed the same thing was true for young doggs, too.

"Like this!" she said, tucking herself into a tight ball and tumbling into the ditch alongside the road.

Oscar imitated her moves as best he could. He also yelped, "Ooo!," "Eee!," and "Ouch!" while he did it. Molly figured rolling around with a chest wound had to hurt.

"Do you think he saw us?" Oscar whispered.

"We'll know soon enough," Molly whispered back.

The dusty pickup truck ground its gears and kept creeping up the steep gravel road.

"He didn't see us!" whispered Molly after the truck passed.

"I have an idea," whispered Oscar. "Did you see any weaselboars riding in the rear cargo bed?"

"No. But I was sort of too busy tucking and rolling to see anything."

Oscar thumped his tail, swishing it through the dirt and gravel. Molly could tell: the dogg was excited.

"If we hopped into the back of that truck, we could ride it up the mountain."

"No way, Oscar. It's too risky."

"No risk, no reward."

"But you're injured."

"Which is why I want to hitch a ride. I have one good sprint left in me, Molly. I want to use it creatively. Come on. Let's do this thing."

"You're crazy," said Molly, reluctantly climbing onto the dogg's back. "You know that, right?"

"Maybe," said Oscar. "But that means you're even crazier. Because you just climbed on my crazy back!"

Molly gripped Oscar's shirt collar. The dogg grunted, clambered out of the ditch, and raced up the road behind the truck. The tailgate of the pickup was hanging open, bouncing and banging and denting itself every time the weaselboar hit a bump.

"If that thing checks its rearview mirror, we're toast!" said Molly, hanging on for dear life as Oscar kept dashing up the rocky road. Even with his injury and his tree-branch crutch, he was fast!

"He's a weaselboar—just like that one who ran into the ravine. Weaselboars never look back. They just charge forward. Hang on! Here we go! Time to take another leap of faith!"

Oscar sprang up off the road and into the back of the pickup truck.

The cargo bed was lined with a thin, moldy carpet.

Molly rolled off Oscar's back, tumbled to the

left, and hugged the side of the truck. Oscar rolled right and hid along the right sidewall.

Molly couldn't believe it.

They'd actually done it. They'd hitched a ride up Crooked Nose Mountain with a weaselboar. The dogg's dumb idea was actually working. They were on their way home! They just had to sit back, relax, and leave the driving to the weaselboar who, hopefully, was on his way to Great Western Park campsite to steal food scraps out of garbage cans or something.

They rambled along for ten full minutes.

Which was when the dumb dogg did something even dumber.

He sat up and scooched his butt along the carpet-lined cargo bed.

"Sorry," he whispered. "I had to."

A roar erupted from the cab of the truck. "Why you little—!"

Apparently, Oscar's butt-scooching had caused the weaselboar to check its rearview mirror.

Chapter 41

The snarling weaselboar slammed the truck to a stop.

Molly and Oscar tumbled forward and squashed against the window of the weaselboar's cab.

The weaselboar whipped around and used its tusks like a battering ram to bash at the glass. The window splintered into rippled veins. Another bash and chunks and shards went flying.

"My bad!" shouted Oscar. "Had an itch. Had to scratch it!"

"You had to get us killed, too!" shouted Molly.

The truck rocked every time the weaselboar smashed into the shattering glass.

Terrified, Oscar and Molly scampered around in circles in the back of the truck, not knowing where to flee next.

"Tuck and roll?" suggested Oscar.

"He can see us, dummy!" said Molly. "If we tuck and roll, he'll just pounce on us!"

Oscar looked up. There were birds of prey circling overhead. He figured they were biding their time, waiting to clean up any carcass scraps the weaselboar left behind after it demolished Oscar and Molly.

There was a loud crash, the tinkle of glass, and an angry snort.

The weaselboar was in the truck bed.

It lowered its head and charged at Oscar.

Oscar dodged the blow. The weaselboar banged into the wooden wall behind him. Hard.

"Good move!" shouted Molly, who was watching Oscar play dodgeball with the weaselboar's tusks from the relative safety of the truck's roof. "Do it again!"

Oscar howled and gave a thumbs-up.

Stumbling slightly from the mild concussion it had given itself, the weaselboar turned around and charged at Oscar again.

This time Oscar leapt up, a split second before the monster could head-butt him. Once again, the weaselboar slammed into the wooden wall of the cargo bed. It staggered and swayed and lurched and tottered.

It made itself the perfect target.

Not for Oscar, but for the big eagles swooping around overhead. A pair dive-bombed the truck, snagged the weaselboar by the scruff of its neck with their sharp talons, and together hauled it up, up and away!

"Woo-hoo!" cried Oscar. "We're still not dead!"

"It's like my father always says," remarked Molly. "Every predator is some other predator's prey."

"But I didn't do it on purpose like you did with the bear and the mountain lion," said Oscar. "I just got lucky."

"So did I!" said Molly. "The day I met you!"

They slapped their paws together and did a quick little dance to celebrate their latest victory.

"So," said Molly. "Do you know how to drive a pickup truck?"

"Nope. But my father has one. I've seen how he does it. You just have to shift gears, goose the gas, turn the steering wheel, and yell at the other drivers on the road because they're all idiots. Easy-fleasy."

"There are no other drivers on this road," said Molly. "It's deserted."

"Fine. We'll skip that part. Come on. We're only halfway up the mountain. And it looks like it's snowing like crazy up there! We better hurry before it turns into a blizzard!"

Chapter 42

Oscar hopped into the pickup truck's driver seat. Molly climbed into the passenger seat.

And then they sat there.

"Um, what exactly are you waiting for?" asked Molly.

"For the motor to start."

"Don't you have to do that?"

"Nope. My father usually does."

"Turn the key," said Molly, rolling her eyes.

Oscar did. The engine whirred and whined and made all sorts of nasty grinding noises.

"You need to take it out of gear first!" shouted Molly.

"I don't know what that means!" Oscar tried sliding the gear shifter knob.

Into Reverse.

The truck rocketed backward.

"Noooo!" shouted Oscar. "We're going the wrong way!"

"Make it go forward!" said Molly.

"How?"

"I don't know!"

They argued all the way down the hill.

Until the truck hit a boulder, rolled sideways, and landed, upside down, in a ditch. The same ditch they had hidden in when they'd first seen the weaselboar's truck.

Oscar and Molly crawled out of the wreckage.

"Owwww, that made my cut feel even worse," said Oscar. He looked at the crushed truck. "Guess we're walking again?"

"Yep," said Molly. "Unless, of course, another truck comes along so you can crash it, too!"

"Are you forgetting that I saved your life?"

"When? Just now when you almost killed me?"

"I meant earlier. When I took care of that weaselboar."

"That wasn't you. That was all eagle."

"So, katt: does your mouth have an Off switch?"

"Nope. But, from what I've seen today, your brain sure does."

After about an hour, they finally stopped arguing. Not because they ran out of katt and dogg insults, but because they were too tired to speak. For the next hour, they grumbled and growled and hissed at each other. Soon, they were too exhausted to do even that.

And they were both cold and hungry.

Very, very hungry.

In fact, by the sixth hour of their grueling hike up the mountain road, they were hungry and confused enough to eat the bark off the trees.

"Dumb dogg," chirped a chipmunk in a nearby clump of shrubs. "Crazy katt. You two will never make it over this mountain alive."

"Chipmunk!" Oscar lunged for the striped rodent, but he was so exhausted he tripped over his own crutch and ended up snout-down in the mud.

The chipmunk cheeped and chipped. "Idiot." Then it scurried away, flicking its tail.

"You two need some serious help," peeped a beautiful silver-gray bird.

Molly's whiskers twitched. "I think I'll help myself...to you!"

She tried to pounce. But her legs felt like they were made out of bricks. She'd lost all her slyness, all her stealth, all her springiness.

When she landed with a wet *splat!* on the spot where the bird used to be, all that was left was a squishy bed of purple berries.

"Gross," she muttered as the berry patch oozed purple juice all over her white fur. Some of the sweet nectar seeped into her mouth.

And it tasted good.

"Woo-hoo!" she shouted joyfully. "Get over here, dogg. We're not dead yet!"

Chapter 43

Oscar limped over to where Molly was sitting in a sea of purple and blue mush.

"It's a whole berry patch!" said Molly. "That bird was trying to help us."

Oscar buried his muzzle in the mess of smooshed berries and lapped up as much purple slop as he could. After he'd gobbled down about a thousand squished berries and his brain started functioning again, he wondered, *Did the bird really do this on purpose? Do birds and animals actually help one another in the Park?*

Maybe that's why he and the katt had been able to get along (for the most part, anyway) out here in the wilderness. The Great Western Frontier Park really was magical, just like everybody said. Even katts and doggs, sworn enemies for life, could get along out here if they tried.

Either that, or this was all one giant coincidence with an order of purple berry mush on the side.

"That bird was so sweet," said Molly, licking some of the purple stains off her paws. "He showed me exactly where to find food! And you said birds hate katts. Ha!"

"They do," said Oscar. "But they *love* doggs. That bird did it for me."

"Wait a second," said Molly. "Aren't some doggs what they call bird doggs? Don't they specifically hunt birds?"

Oscar shrugged. "Not any of my relatives. We're squirrel doggs. And chipmunk doggs. And bacon doggs..."

Molly laughed. Oscar did, too. Having a full belly made it easy to laugh again.

"Ready to hike up the hill?" asked Oscar.

"Totally," said Molly. "We should pack up some of these berries."

Oscar nodded eagerly. "Definitely. They taste much better than tree bark."

The dogg and katt continued climbing toward the peak of Crooked Nose Mountain. When they reached an elevation where the only trees were evergreens, a light flurry of snow started to swirl around them. As they hiked higher, the snowfall became heavier.

Chapter 44

When night fell, Oscar and Molly decided to stop hiking.

"It's kind of hard to see where we're going in the dark with all this snow," said Oscar. "I can't smell much, either. The cold and ice have covered up all the scents."

"Well, let's make camp under that big tree," said Molly. "There's a nice bed of soft needles around the trunk. And the evergreen branches are like a canopy to keep out the snow."

Oscar was able to bang together some rock

shards he'd found in the roadway and spark a campfire. Molly was in charge of fluffing the pine needles and thawing the berries.

They huddled around the crackling blaze and shivered together against the still swirling wind and snow.

"Tomorrow," said Oscar, "once we pass over the peak, it'll all be downhill so we'll move faster."

"Good," said Molly. "I can't wait to get home. I've missed so many acting classes."

"How come you want to be an actress?"

"I like pretending to be characters who aren't really me. Then I can act like someone who isn't my mother and father's daughter. When I'm playing a part in a play, I don't have to do things exactly the way my parents want me to. I can be my own katt."

"By pretending to be someone else?"

"Exactly! Besides, ever since I was a kitten, everybody's told me I could be a movie star. I've got the looks for it. And the eyes."

She batted her sparkling baby blues at Oscar.

"They're like the sky," he said. "Only bluer."

"I know," said Molly. "It's a gift. How about you? What's the first thing you're going to do when you get home?"

"Well, first I'll eat a big, delicious dinner. Something besides berries."

"Yeah. Tuna fish wrapped in mackerel!"

"Nope. A double bacon cheeseburger, extra cheese, hold the bun! Then, I'll go back into training. Not to brag..."

"Go ahead. Brag."

"Okay. Coach says I'm the best young athlete in all of Doggsylvania!"

"Well, I know for a fact you're an excellent runner."

"Yeah. It's my top sport. Running and fetching. I'm on the fetching team, too."

Molly sighed. "I miss my mom."

"I'm glad she's a nurse," said Oscar. "My mom's a nurse, too."

"No way."

"Way. Next time, I'll pay more attention when she tells me about medicinal herbs and where to find them."

As the night wore on, they swapped all sorts of stories.

About their schools. And their favorite places to hang out back home. And food. When you're hungry, with nothing but purple berries in your belly, food is always a very hot topic. But mostly they talked about how much they missed and loved their families, even their fathers, who could both be kind of grumpy and grouchy.

"It's just his way," said Oscar.

"I know what you mean," said Molly. "I've got the same deal with my dad."

Oscar stared at Molly. "You're still a katt, right?"

"Uh, yeah."

"And I'm still a dogg?"

"Definitely."

"Then how come we have so much in common?"

Molly shrugged. "I have no idea."

"Yeah," said Oscar. "Me, neither. I guess that's something else we have in common."

Chapter 45

Molly and Oscar rose with the sun.

They'd taken turns staying awake throughout the night to guard each other. But even when it was one of their turns to sleep, they didn't do much of it. The night was too cold. They were both too terrified of all the dangers lurking in the darkness.

"You ready to climb to the summit?" asked Molly as Oscar slowly creaked up from the bed of pine needles and leaned against his crutch.

"You betcha," he said cheerily, even though his

tail was drooping between his legs.

Molly could tell: The dogg was in a great deal of pain. But, he limped on.

The higher they climbed, the deeper the snow.

"We're topping out!" exclaimed Molly when she could see blue sky through the stand of trees. "We made it! It's all downhill from here."

Molly ran and Oscar hobbled across the peak of Crooked Nose Mountain to a switchback trail on the other side. The air was crisp and crystal clear. You could see for miles in every direction.

"Look!" said Molly. "Way off in the distance. That's the entrance to the Western Frontier Park!"

"Where?"

"That smudge down there. On the far side of the wide, winding river."

"I see it, I see it!" said Oscar, wagging his tail and panting eagerly. "That's the road we took. The highway."

They were so high up they could even see the hazy outlines of Kattsburgh and Doggsylvania, far off in the distance.

"Last one down the mountain is a rotten can of

sardines!" said Molly, ready to run.

"Hey!" said Oscar with a laugh, hobbling after her. "No fair. I'm still on the injured reserve list, here!"

"Fine. We should sled down!"

"Great idea," said Oscar. "We could lash together a bunch of tree limbs and branches. Or we could make two pairs of snowshoes and—"

"Aiieeeeee!" screamed Molly.

An eagle had just swooped down and plucked her off of the bluff!

"Help!" screamed Molly as she struggled in midair.

Oscar dashed down the trail, following the bird and his friend. "Hang on!" he shouted.

"I can't! The eagle's hanging on to *me*. I'm hooked in its talons!"

The eagle swerved sharply, following the curving stone wall lining the road.

Molly figured this was one way to climb down the mountain fast: in the clutches of a crazed bird bringing food home to its hungry babies.

The eagle made another hairpin turn, hugging the side of the W-shaped road.

And Molly saw Oscar.

He had leapt from one stone wall to the next and caught up with the bird.

The dogg flew up off his rocky perch and grabbed Molly's legs with his arms. The combined weight of the katt and dogg was too much for the eagle. It started to lose speed and altitude fast.

"Let us go, birdbrain!" shouted Oscar, sounding a lot like his dad. "Or you're going to crash into that rock down there."

That's when the eagle let go.

Molly and Oscar were falling.

"Thanks, dogg!" said Molly as they whizzed toward the jagged rocks on the ground below. "It was nice knowing you."

"Likewise!" said Oscar.

And then they both crashed.

Chapter 46

They landed in a soft snow bank six inches away from the sharp rocks.

"We're still not dead!" Oscar shouted. "Woo-hoo!"

Molly was hugging him tightly. She wouldn't let go.

So, Oscar hugged her back.

O-kay, he thought. *This is totally embarrassing. I'm hugging a katt. In a snowdrift. Un-be-liev-able. I'm glad Dad isn't here to see this! She is kind of soft and cuddly, though…*

He didn't say anything out loud, of course. He just held on to Molly and let her say, "Thank you, thank you, thank you" a million times in a row.

"You're welcome," said Oscar, still not breaking the hug, because they'd landed in a mound of snow and two bodies are always warmer than one.

"Remember when I said you reminded me of my brother?" said Molly.

"Yeah. Because I'm so easily distracted."

"Well, that's not the only reason. Not anymore."

"Okay. What's the new reason?"

"You're like the best kind of brother, Oscar. Somebody who'll look out for me, no matter what. Someone willing to jump up at an eagle and risk his own life to save mine!"

"You did that for me, Molly. When you came back with the medicine and stuff..."

"Huh. I guess that makes me your sister."

"Kind of, sort of," said Oscar. "Temporarily. Until we get home. That was our deal."

"Right," said Molly. "Of course."

The snow was cold. More was falling. Oscar

and Molly huddled closer together.

"Well, ain't this groovy?" boomed a jolly voice.

A snowy white bear was standing over Oscar and Molly, grinning like crazy. She wore a necklace of woven flowers draped around her neck.

Oscar and Molly sprang out of their cuddle, stirring up all sorts of frosty snow. Oscar put up his paws, ready to defend himself and Molly from the huge bear. It wasn't wearing clothes so it must be one of the wild, savage ones.

The bear leaned down closer and opened her mouth wide.

Oscar bravely stood snout-to-snout with the beast. Maybe he could scare it off before it ate them? He had to try!

But the bear's mouth curved into a grin. "Are you two, like, boyfriend and girlfriend, man?" she asked.

"What?" said Oscar.

"No way," said Molly.

"We're like brother and sister!" said Oscar defensively.

"Or sister and brother," said Molly.

"Really?" said the snowy white bear. "Well, heh-heh-heh, that's even funnier, man. A katt and a dogg? Brother and sister? Far out. That's what this world needs more of, baby. Love, sweet love."

Oscar stood up and dusted off some snow. Molly did the same thing.

"We're not in love," said Oscar.

"Being in love is gross," said Molly.

"You can *love* without being *in* love, man," said the polar bear. "Can you dig what I'm laying down, children?"

"Sure," said Molly. "Whatever. We just want to get home."

"Far out," said the polar bear. "Where do you two lovebirds call home?"

"We are *not* lovebirds!" insisted Molly.

"I'm a dogg, she's a katt," added Oscar. "Neither one of us is remotely related to birds..."

"And doggs and katts hate each other," said Molly.

"Is that so?" chuckled the big bear. "Oh, right. I heard about that. Whole lot of hating going on down in the big cities. It's why my family moved to the country, man. Too many haters in the city. Couldn't handle all those negative vibes."

"I'm from Doggsylvania," said Oscar.

"Kattsburgh," said Molly. "Do you know how to get there?"

"Nope. Sorry. But I do know how to get down off this mountain and into the Western Frontier Park."

Oscar gave that a hearty arm pump. "Yes! We are going home, Molly! Home!"

"So, what are your names?" asked the polar bear.

"I'm Oscar."

"Molly."

The bear chuckled again. (She chuckled a lot.) "Oscar and Molly, sitting in a tree, k-i-s—"

"We were not sitting in a tree!" insisted Molly, because she knew what the next part of the rhyme would be.

"We were sitting in the snow!" added Oscar.

"I know, man," said the bear. "You were cuddling and snuggling."

"Because we were cold!" said Molly.

"Far out. By the way, my name's Momsy."

"Seriously?" Oscar and Molly said at the same time.

"Yep. For reals. Climb on my back, little bro and sis. It's time to get down and boogie—all the way to the valley below."

Oscar and Molly didn't hesitate. They quickly grabbed a handful of Momsy's fluffy fur, hauled themselves up onto her back, and snuggled down into her soft and cozy warmth.

"This is way better than a pickup truck," whispered Molly.

"You got that right," Oscar whispered back.

And they spent the day riding in plush comfort down the far side of Crooked Nose Mountain.

Chapter 47

That same morning, in Faunae City, where the United Federation of Animals kept its capitol, the head magistrate, a hippopotamus in black robes, was listening to complaints from his constituents.

"The beavers dammed up the darn river again!" complained a raccoon. "This has seriously endangered our ancestral fishing grounds."

"Is this true?" the wise hippo asked a beaver with sawdust flaking like dandruff on his dark suit.

"Yes, sir, your majesty," said the buck-toothed beaver.

"I'm a magistrate, not a majesty."

"Oh. Sorry. Want a toothpick? I just nibbled one out of this chair leg..."

The hippo banged his gavel.

Startled, the beaver stopped chewing the furniture.

The raccoon nervously fiddled with his fingers under his chin.

"Hear ye, hear ye," declared the magistrate. "Henceforth, the raccoons shall fish on the upstream side of the beaver dam instead of the downstream side."

"Oh," said the raccoon. "Good idea, sir. Wonder why I didn't think of that?"

"Because," said the hippo, "you were too busy being mad at the beavers to think up a sensible compromise. Next case?"

The katt and dogg families pushed their way to the front of the room. A clump of reporters and camera people pushed forward with them.

"Your honor, sir," said Oscar's father, Duke.

"Pardon my pun, but we got us a real kattastrophe on our hands here."

"Oh, go step in a poodle," hissed Boomer, Molly's father.

"My wife's part poodle!" snapped Duke.

"Fine," sniffed Boomer. "Step on her."

"Why, I oughtta…" Oscar's dad balled up his paw into a fist.

The hippo hammered his gavel. "Enough!

You're the families of the two missing children, correct?"

"That's right, chief," said Duke. "And that lame hawkowl ranger you people have working at your Western Frontier Park hasn't done diddly to find my son."

"However," added Boomer, "she's done an even worse job locating *my* lost daughter!"

"We need money to continue the search," said the dogg. "We have to pull out all the stops, and organize the biggest rescue effort we can. Will you give us what we need?"

The hippo gave him a stern look. "The rangers are doing all they can to help locate your child."

Oscar's father growled. "We need double the helicopters and triple the people to find Oscar!"

"What about Molly?" demanded the katt.

"Ah, nobody cares about her."

"What? How dare you, you poop-sniffing excuse for an animal being!"

The hippo banged his gavel some more. "Order! Order in the court."

"I'll take a tuna burger with a side of salmon fries," shouted Blade.

"You see how, like, totally stupid these katts are?" huffed Fifi.

The paparazzi—the news crews and freelance photographers who followed the katt and dogg families everywhere they went—snapped pictures and filmed video clips. The ferret reporter was jumping up and down with glee. She'd have some excellent dogg-versus-katt action footage for that night's tabloid TV show.

The dogg and katt families kept hurling insults at each other. Then they started throwing punches. Pretty soon, teeth and claws were involved.

"Good thing I'm a nurse!" shouted both of the mothers at the same time.

The hippo banged his gavel again. Nobody paid attention to him. The doggs and katts were at one another's throats. The fur was flying!

"You katts and doggs are impossible! Request *denied!*" shouted the hippo over all the barking, hissing, snarling, and screeching. "Bailiffs! Clear the room!"

Five burly guards—four big gorillas aided by an elephant—came in and broke up the dogg and katt fight.

There would be no last-ditch rescue mission.

Oscar and Molly were, officially, on their own.

Chapter 48

Well, here we are, dude and dudette!" said Momsy, the blubbery polar bear. "The Mighty Big River. Your so-called civilization is right over there on the other side."

Oscar slid down the bear's white fleecy fur and landed on the ground. Molly slid down after him. On the far shore of the churning, choppy water, they could see a road and buildings. They were so close to going home!

"The river's too broad," said Oscar.

"Nah, man," said Momsy. "It's just mighty and big."

"That water is at least a half mile wide!" said Molly.

"For sure," said Momsy.

"We'll never make it across," said Oscar. "I can't doggy paddle that far with a katt on my back. Not through raging rapids!"

"Probably not, man," said Momsy. "But then, again, why would you want to?"

"Because," said Molly defensively, "we're kind of, sort of on this journey together."

"That's right," said Oscar. "We're temporarily, kind of, sort of helping each other. A little."

"I can dig it," said Momsy. "But, I mean, why would you want to go back *there*, man? There's nothing on the far shore but haters. Dogg hates katt. Katt hates dogg. And so on and so on and doo-bee-doo-bee-doo."

"Whaaat?" said Oscar.

"Nothin', dude. Just a song we sometimes sing out here in the Park. It's also the reason why I never want to set paw in the city. Yours or hers."

"But how do we get across this river?" asked Molly.

The bear shrugged. "Don't know. Never *tried* to do it because I never *wanted* to do it. Ciao, for now. You're on your own, kids. I'm outta here."

The big bear lumbered away, singing, "'Many rivers to cross...'"

"We're just worried about this one!" Molly shouted after her.

The bear kept walking away, singing her song, tossing a two-finger peace sign over her shoulder.

"Thank you for the ride!" Oscar shouted. To Molly, he said, "She's wrong. We are not on our own. We're together."

"Correct," said Molly. "Because we're *stuck* together on this side of the river when we want to be on that side!"

"Well," said Oscar, nervously wagging his tail, "we just need to figure this thing out."

"Fine." Molly started licking her paws.

"Um, what are you doing, Molly?"

"Licking my paws. It helps me think."

"Good idea." Oscar hunkered down into a prone

position. "I do my best thinking in pre-pounce mode."

The two of them stared at the river. And the far shore. And the logs and branches whizzing downstream in the roiling rapids.

"If only we had a raft," said Oscar.

"Yeah," said Molly.

Just then they saw a beaver floating down the river, riding on a log.

Molly looked at Oscar. Oscar looked at Molly.

"We need help!" they said together.

"But it's wild," Molly said.

"That didn't stop Momsy or Granny from help-ing us," Oscar pointed out.

Molly nodded and they waved at the beaver, jumping up and down on the riverbank.

Then, together, they screamed: *"Help!"*

Chapter 49

Hey, buddy!" Oscar barked at the beaver. "Over here!"

The buck-toothed drifter floated closer to the shore.

"Oh, my," he said in a funny, nasal voice. "A dogg and a katt? Together? That's hysterical!"

"It's temporary," said Molly.

"Yep. Sure it is," said the beaver. "Yep, yep, yep."

He let go of his log and scampered up the river-bank to join Oscar and Molly, where he gave his wet coat a hearty shake to dry off.

"Ewww," said Molly, when dirty beaver water splattered all over her formerly white fur.

"Sorry about that," said the beaver, flopping his tail up and down. "So, you folks need help?"

"Yeah," said Oscar. "And logs. Lots and lots of logs."

"We want to build a raft," said Molly.

"Interesting," said the beaver. "Never built one, myself, but I've seen 'em. I mostly build dams and other infrastructure projects."

"Well," said Oscar, "maybe if you can cut down some trees, someone else will help us lash them together?"

"Oh, yeah. Sure. That could happen. Yep, yep, yep. On this side of the river, anyways. Over here, we're still in the Western Frontier Park where everybody goes along to get along. We keep the peace. Over there in civilization? Not so much. Stand back. You folks want logs, I've got some chewin' to be doin'."

The beaver attacked a stand of medium-sized trees with his buzz-saw mouth. Sawdust and wood chips went flying everywhere.

"Tim-berrr!" hollered the beaver. Trees toppled like falling dominoes.

"How many logs you folks need?" the beaver asked with a toothy grin after the fourth tree crashed to the ground. He had wood chunks between his front teeth.

"Um, how about one more?" said Oscar.

"Sure. No problem. Chew it down in a jiffy."

"But how are we going to tie them all together?" asked Molly.

"Easy peasy," said the beaver. "You just need a monkey."

"Huh?" said Oscar.

"A chimp," said the beaver. "They swing on vines around here all the time." He whistled through his teeth. Two long blasts followed by two short tweets.

A monkey came swinging out of the forest behind them.

"What's up?" asked the monkey.

"Chewin' wood. Helpin' some strangers. Same old, same old."

"I'm down with that," said the monkey, turning to Oscar and Molly. "What do you folks need?"

"Some ropey vines," said Oscar. "To tie these logs together."

The monkey nodded his head. "Makin' a raft, huh?"

"Yes," said Molly. "We're lost and need to go home."

"And home's on the other side of the river," added Oscar.

"Kattsburgh? Doggsylvania?" said the monkey,

as she started yanking ropey vines out of the trees.

"That's right," said Oscar.

"I have a cousin in Baboonville," said the monkey. "Visited once. Didn't like it. The baboons hate the monkeys who hate the gibbons who hate the chimps. If I were you two, I'd stay over here in the Park. We're a lot more chill over here."

"But over there is home," said Oscar.

"Whatever," said the monkey. "Grab some vine, kid."

The two of them dragged the vines over to where the logs were lined up next to one another.

"Now we need someone good at lashing."

"I can do that," said Oscar. "I'm a Dogg Scout."

"I'll help," said Molly. "I'm good at playing with yarn."

Oscar and Molly wove several strands of vines up and under and up and around the logs. The monkey tied the ends into knots. The beaver trimmed off the dangling end pieces.

In no time, the four of them had built a raft.

"Now you just need a riverboat pilot," said the monkey.

"Yep, yep, yep," said the beaver. "You need Old Jim."

He whistled through his teeth. A long-short-long-short tweet.

An ancient otter surfaced in the river. "Someone call my name?"

Chapter 50

Y ou two lookin' to slip over to the other side?" asked Old Jim the otter.

"We need to go home," said Molly, dramatically. "I've been in the wilderness so long, my fur looks like something the katt dragged in!"

"I miss my mother!" said Oscar, before he could catch himself. "And, you know, my whole family."

"Well, climb aboard the raft, children, and I'll pilot you on over to the other side, I reckon," said Old Jim. "I love a-sliding down the big river. We can catch fish and talk, and take a swim now and then to keep off sleepiness."

"We just want to go across," said Molly.

Old Jim shrugged. "Suit yourself, missy. But it's kind of solemn, drifting down the big, still river, laying on your backs looking up at the stars."

Molly thought the otter's words sounded like something out of a book. "Thanks, Mr. Old Jim. Maybe we can do that with you later, but right now, we just want to go home to our families," she said sweetly.

Oscar nodded, his tongue hanging out of his mouth.

"Then I won't try to convince you otherwise," said the otter. "One thing I've learned is never try to teach a pig to sing. You waste your time and you annoy the pig."

"Um, neither one of us is a pig," said Oscar.

"It's a metaphor, son. Work with me."

Molly turned to the beaver. "Are you sure this old coot of an otter is the best riverboat captain we can find?" she whispered, shielding her mouth with a paw.

"The best," said the beaver, eagerly.

"Okay," said Molly. "Let's launch this thing!"

Molly, Oscar, the beaver, and the monkey worked together to shove the lashed logs into the rippling water. Old Jim steadied the raft in place with his paws.

"Best climb aboard, children," said Old Jim. "River sometimes has a mind of its own. Might take you where it wants to go instead of where you want to go."

Oscar and Molly leapt onto the bumpy logs of the wobbly rivercraft. They called out their thanks and waved good-bye to the kind beaver and monkey. Wild animals were so much kinder than civilized ones!

"Next stop, the far side!" said the ancient otter, shoving off from the shore. Then he started whistling to himself.

Old Jim kept blathering on about the Mighty Big River but he also kept flipping his tail like crazy. The ancient otter was so incredibly strong he was able to pilot the raft across the river, through the swift current, even while he waxed poetic on all manner of subjects.

"I speak true, children," said Old Jim, as they rolled over the rapids, "I have seen doggs good and doggs bad. I've seen katts good and katts bad. This here river is what separates 'em."

"What about deer?" asked Molly. "Have you seen good deer, too?"

"I reckon I have, by and by."

"Well how about that guy on the shore," said Oscar, pointing at the giant creature with an enormous set of antlers that remind him of a dogg coat

245

rack. The deer was fully clothed in plaid flannel and blue jeans. That meant he wasn't wild. "His antlers would make a good place for us to tie off!"

"But is he a good deer?" asked Molly. "Or a bad one?"

"Only one way to find out, I reckon," said Old Jim. "Toss him a line!"

Chapter 51

Oscar grabbed a clump of coiled vine with his teeth.

He whipped his head sideways to heave the ropey thing up to the deer standing on the shoreline.

The deer dipped his head.

The vine whipped around and around his antlers like a bolo.

"I charge a docking fee," the deer snorted, once the rope line was tied off, taut and secure.

"Civilization," grumbled Old Jim, treading water

at the rear of the raft. "That's what folks call it on this side of the river. I'll stay on my side where I reckon kindness don't have a price."

"Civilization is where we live," said Oscar. "Come on, Molly. Let's go home."

"Um, how are we going to pay the deer the docking fee?"

Oscar had to think about that for a second. "I know! By letting him be the one who rescues us! I'm sure there's a reward."

"True. My father is extremely rich. And I'm his Priceless Princess."

"Seriously?"

"It's sort of a nickname. Come on, dogg. I don't know about you, but I'm in a hurry to get home. It'll be so good to sleep in my own bed and poop in my own litter box!"

The nimble little katt sprang off the raft and landed on the riverbank.

Oscar, on the other hand, needed to go to the rear of the raft so he could take a running start before leaping. Old Jim was in the river, looking up at Oscar and shaking his head.

"Good luck, dogg. I have a feeling you're gonna need it. Up there in the civilized world, animal beings can be awful cruel to one another."

"Yeah," said Oscar. "It's sort of what we do. Thanks for the ride!"

He exploded into a sprint and flew off the edge of the raft.

"Woo-hoo!" he shouted when his paws touched ground. "Nailed that landing, big time."

"See you next time, children," said Old Jim, shoving off from the shore with the raft.

"Thank you, Old Jim! We'll come back and pay you when we have money!" said Molly.

"I do not wish any reward but to know I have done the right thing," called the otter as he floated away.

The deer held up a hoof. "I'm not a dumb beast like the otter. Where's my docking fee, kids?"

"It's coming," said Molly distractedly.

"So's Christmas."

"You just have to give us a ride."

"What?"

"You want your money, right?"

249

"Uh, duh," said the deer.

"Then take me to my daddy!" Molly pointed to the billboard she'd been admiring ever since she sprang off the raft and saw it.

BRING HOME MOLLY! BIG REWARD $$$! screamed the headline over her favorite glam shot.

Someone had added a new banner to the billboard: BIG RALLY AT CAPITOL TODAY!

"My dad paid for that billboard," said Molly. "He's Boomer Hissleton the Third. Ever heard of him?"

"Yeah," said the deer. "Everybody's heard of him. He's rich and on TV!"

"Well Molly here is his 'Priceless Princess'!" added Oscar.

"Is that so?" said the deer.

Molly gave him her most regal look. "It most certainly is."

"Then climb aboard, Princess. I'll happily haul you home."

"Um, what about me?" said Oscar.

The deer looked to Molly. She nodded.

"You have to haul him, too," she said. "We're still kind of, sort of in this thing together."

Chapter 52

At that very moment, Boomer Hissleton the Third, Esquire, was addressing a crowd on the steps of the capitol building in Faunae City.

"My fellow katts," he said into a bank of microphones. "My darling daughter needs your help. She has been lost in the wilderness for days. She has, undoubtedly, faced all sorts of gruesome, dangerous foes, including..."

Molly's father's shoulders heaved and lurched. Repeatedly. The thought of what he was about to say next was making him feel as if he had to hock up a hairball.

"A dastardly, dangerous *dogg!*" he blurted, spitting out the horrible word as if it were a soggy lump of semi-digested fur.

The five or six katts in the crowd hissed. The lion, tiger, and panther growled. The crowd outside the capitol building that morning was woefully thin and sparse. Molly had been missing for so long, she was rapidly becoming yesterday's news. Not that many creatures were still interested in her plight. They'd moved on to the next big story. Something about a gerbil.

"We need to raise more money to raise a rescue team!" Molly's father continued. "Please dig deep! Give whatever you can!"

That's when the katts and other feline creatures in the crowd started coughing. And remembering they had previous appointments. And casually strolling away.

"Step aside," Oscar's dad snarled to Molly's father as he made his way to the microphones.

"Forget about the katt, everybody. She's probably dead, anyway."

"I beg your pardon?" snapped Boomer, Molly's father.

Duke shrugged. "She's a katt. What do katts know about fending for themselves? They always want somebody to wait on them and bring them din-din in dainty little crystal dishes."

"I'll have you know, you slobbering oaf, we katts are some of the finest hunters on the planet."

"You mean you used to be. Now you're soft and lazy. You spend most of your day napping. My son, Oscar? He's a Dogg Scout. An athlete. He knows how to survive in the wilderness. Even has a badge for it. So, if you folks want to give money to a rescue party, give it to the party who still has a chance of being rescued. My son, Oscar."

"Molly is important, too!" hissed her father.

"Not to me, she isn't!" growled Duke.

"Molly needs your help!" her father pleaded with what was left of the crowd, which was one elephant. He was so humongous and slow, it took him longer than everybody else to turn his back on the bickering dogg and katt.

"Oscar needs it more!" Duke shouted at the lumbering elephant.

"Does not!"

"Does, too!"

"Doesn't!

"Does!"

Finally, the elephant flung up its trunk in disgust and trumpeted a wet "Shaddap!" over its shoulder. As the elephant turned, when its wide rear end was no longer blocking the view, both Duke and Boomer saw something miraculous riding toward them on the back of a deer.

Oscar and Molly!

Chapter 53

"Lola!" screamed Duke. "Fifi! Get out here. Oscar's come home!"

Oscar's mother and sister came running out of the capitol building and down the steps. So did Molly's mother and brother.

"Hiya, Mom. Blade!" said Molly. "Hey, Dad!"

"Hallelujah!" shouted Boomer. "My daughter is alive!"

"So's my son!" shouted Duke. "And he looks more alive than your daughter ever could!"

The two families knocked over the stand of

microphones and raced to the bottom of the steps where the deer stood with their children. Before long, Oscar's whole family was hugging him while Molly's whole family was hugging her.

"You're safe!" both mothers sobbed at the same time.

"You can have all your squeaky toys back," said Oscar's sister, Fifi.

"Thanks," said Oscar.

"Ahem," said the deer. "I believe youse owe me a reward for finding these two?"

Molly's father hesitated.

"Since you rescued both my daughter and this, this...dogg child...I think I can only be held responsible for *half* of the reward. The mangy mutt's family can pay you the rest."

"You know, katt, you must've been born on a highway," snapped Oscar's dad. "Because that's where most accidents happen. No way am I paying this deer diddly. We never offered a reward. That was all you."

"Because I love my daughter more than you love your son!"

"Says who?"

"Me. Weren't you listening? Must be hard with those big floppy ears of yours barely poking out of that grimy cap!" Boomer hissed.

"Why, I oughtta..." snarled Duke, flaring his fangs.

"Yo," screamed the deer. "I want my reward money!"

"Pay him, Daddy," said Molly.

"Fine," said Boomer, writing a check for a large sum of money.

The deer snorted and took off. The katts hugged Molly some more. The doggs patted Oscar on the back.

"It's so good to have you home, Molly," said Boomer. Then he noticed that Molly was missing the tip of her tail and the top of one ear. He spun around and hissed at Oscar. "Did you do this to my daughter, you dirty, disgusting dogg?"

"No, sir," said Oscar. "She was like that when I first met her. I didn't do it. Tell him, Molly."

Molly looked to her father. She wanted to say something to defend Oscar.

But her father looked so angry and full of hate that she didn't.

She didn't mention the mountain lion. She didn't say anything about the other hardships they'd endured together. She just stood frozen, looking scared while her father (and pretty soon her mother and brother) hissed at Oscar.

That hurt Oscar—maybe even more than the

weaselboar tusk slashing across his chest.

"Whoa, whoa, whoa," said Oscar's dad. "What's that big cut on your chest, there, Oscar? Did that creepy katt slash you with her claws?"

Oscar looked at Molly who still wasn't saying anything to defend him.

So he returned the favor.

He didn't say anything to defend her, either!

Chapter 54

With the safe return of Oscar and Molly, you might assume that things would change in Kattsburgh and Doggsylvania.

You might suppose that Oscar and Molly's feuding families would have a change of heart after they heard the truth about how their two children helped each other survive in the wilderness.

You might even imagine that the wise words about animal unity from the head park ranger would ring throughout the civilized land.

You might assume, suppose, and imagine all that. But you'd be wrong.

The katts and doggs were still at each other's throats, spreading rumors and lies.

Oscar sat in his dogg bed flipping through the TV channels. One news station said he was a hero for surviving the "horrible and horrendous hardships" of the wilderness as only "a true Dogg Scout could."

On another 24-hour news channel—one that featured mostly katt food, kattnip, and feather toy commercials—the katt commentators in their squares and boxes kept yelling at each other, insisting that Oscar should be locked up in the dogg pound.

The same thing was true on the internet. Pro-dogg websites cast Oscar as a hero and Molly as a villain. They blamed the katt for Oscar's wounds.

Pro-katt sites called Oscar a mutt, a mongrel, and a menace to society. They blamed him for everything from ticks to fleas to Molly's nipped ear, which might "seriously jeopardize her dreams of becoming a famous feline movie star."

Oscar sighed and remembered how Molly had helped him when he was hurt. How she brought him all those medicinal herbs.

Oscar hadn't seen Molly since the day they returned home. But he'd never forget their time together in the scary wilderness. How they helped each other. How they kept each other safe. How they kind of, sort of, temporarily became friends.

He'd never tell his family, the TV and newspaper reporters, or even the bloggers but, secretly, he missed her.

He missed her a lot.

Chapter 55

Molly was napping in a sunny spot in the living room when she heard the doorbell ring.

"Where's Molly?" asked whoever was at the front door. "Where's our next big TV star?"

Molly sprang up and groomed herself with a few quick paw licks.

"There she is!"

The ferret Molly recognized from the Weasel Broadcasting Network on cable TV burst into the living room.

"Oh, my! Those eyes! They're amazing! They're

so blue they could be swimming pools. No. They could be the sky. No. The sky reflected in a swimming pool!"

"How may I be of assistance?" asked Molly, using super excellent diction to pronounce all the syllables.

"By letting me make you a star, Molly!" said the ferret. "We've been covering your struggle out in the wilderness. All the trials and tribulations of being stranded with your Sworn Enemy for Life. Now, we want to host a live, must-see TV event."

"What's all this?" said Molly's dad as he strolled into the living room.

"Mr. Hissleton," said the ferret. "We've met."

"Indeed, we have," said Boomer. "I never forget a ferret. You're the TV reporter."

"That's right. I'm also ready to take Molly's fame to the next level."

"Really?" Molly giggled. "Tell me more."

"You got it, kiddo. Let me put this on the stoop and see if you folks lick it up."

The ferret rubbed her paws together.

"The Weasel Broadcasting Network wants to

host a one-on-one, live debate between you and your sworn enemy, Oscar," said the ferret. "You two will confront each other at the city auditorium. I'll moderate. You can finally tell the whole world the truth about that demented and dangerous dogg."

"It'll be ugly!" said Molly's father.

"And that's why it will be so beautiful," said the ferret. "Molly will demolish Oscar. Live on national television. Everybody will be watching: doggs, katts, monkeys, gerbils, hyenas. Even the fish will tune in for this."

"Molly," gushed her mom, "this is the big break you've been waiting for all your life. After this live TV debate, you'll be famous!"

"This is your shot, dear," said Boomer. "If you want to be a movie star, this will put you miles ahead of the competition."

The ferret pulled out a long scroll filled with legal mumbo jumbo.

"I need you to sign this contract on your daughter's behalf, Mr. Hissleton," she said.

Boomer Hissleton looked at his daughter. "Do you want to be a star, Molly?"

It was what she'd wanted her entire life. Molly nodded. "Do it, Daddy," she said.

Then she grinned. She was going to be famous.

Chapter 56

Ten minutes later, the WBN ferret was at Oscar's house.

"Let me put this in your bowl and see if you folks gobble it down," she said, launching into the same sales pitch she'd made to the katts.

"You two will confront each other at the city auditorium," said the ferret. "I'll moderate. The whole thing goes out live—on TV, the internet, everywhere. You can finally tell the whole world the truth about that crazed, chest-slashing katt, Molly."

"It'll get so nasty!" said his father.

"And that's why it will be so beautiful," said the ferret. "Oscar will totally demolish Molly. Live on national television. There will no longer be any question about who's the superior species. Doggs will rule and katts will drool."

"Actually," said Oscar, "we're sort of the droolers. Katts mostly purr and lick their paws and…"

"Son?" said his father. "Have you gone soft on me?"

"No, sir. It's just that the ferret said—"

"Did I mention that we're paying?" asked the ferret.

"You mean money?" asked Oscar's dad.

"Yes, sir. Unless you'd rather have kibble?"

"No, money's fine. Money's good."

"We like money," said Oscar's sister.

"How much are we talking about here?" asked Oscar's dad.

"Well, sir," said the ferret, "if you sign on the dotted line today, I am authorized by my network to guarantee you a minimum of fifty thousand against a ceiling of one hundred thousand!"

Oscar's father whistled. When he did, all the other doggs perked up one ear.

The ferret unfurled a scroll with all sorts of legal mumbo jumbo written on it.

"I don't like this idea," said Oscar. In fact, he totally hated it.

"What part don't you like?" asked his father, puffing out his chest. "Destroying those snooty

273

katts once and for all or the money we're going to make doing it?"

"We do need the money, sweetheart," added his mother.

"I know I totally do," said his sister.

"Well, Oscar?" said his father, glaring at him.

Oscar thought about Molly. Then he thought about the money. And then he remembered how Molly didn't defend him when her father accused Oscar of nipping off the tip of her tail and ear.

Molly never really was his friend, was she?

She was just a katt.

A sneaky, stuck-up, hissy-fit-throwing katt.

"Sign the contract, Dad," he said. "Let's do this thing!"

Chapter 57

On the night of the big debate, Oscar rode to the city auditorium in the back of his father's pickup truck.

Searchlights crisscrossed the sky above the city auditorium. Oscar's father needed a police escort to make his way through the snarled traffic. It seemed as though every dogg and every katt in the land was coming to see the big show.

The pressure was so intense that Oscar was feeling sick to his stomach. The can of nacho-flavored

Chunkee Stuff he'd had for dinner was probably a mistake, too.

"Look at all those doggs, Oscar!" his dad shouted from the cab of the truck when they pulled up outside the auditorium. "They're all here for you, son!"

Oscar saw a mob of rowdy doggs—stacked six deep—lined up behind a velvet rope on one side of a long red carpet. A mob of katts—just as deep and vicious—was lined up along the other side. The two sides were snarling, hissing, and swatting at each other. Security guards, mostly baboons, were keeping the crowd under control.

Everybody had their cell phones up to snap pictures of the two combatants' big arrival. The TV ferret was there with her blazing lights and camera crew, ready to interview Oscar and Molly.

"Oh, great," grumbled Oscar's dad as the truck lurched to a stop. "We have to wait for *them*!"

"Now, dear, don't start foaming at the mouth," said Oscar's mom. "Everybody will think you have rabies..."

"Who cares? I'm ticked off, Lola. How come those katts get to go into the auditorium first?"

"Maybe because Molly is so pretty!" gushed Oscar's sister, when she saw Molly step into the camera light with the ferret reporter.

Oscar had to agree: Molly was looking magnificent.

Her white coat was clean and shiny. Then again, it was the first time Oscar had ever seen it without mud streaks or clumps of sticky-bush burrs buried in it. Her blue, blue eyes had never been more brilliant and clear.

Molly looked exactly like the movie star she'd told Oscar she would become one day.

Well, that day was today.

Oscar was so happy for her, he almost started kicking his leg the way he did whenever somebody tickled the happy spot on his belly.

Because (don't tell his parents or any other dogg), to his surprise, he was actually proud of Molly!

Chapter 58

Yes," Molly said to the ferret after making sure the TV camera was aimed at her best side. "I'm really looking forward to this evening. It should prove highly entertaining."

"Will you tear into your opponent with both claws?" asked the ferret.

"I prefer to employ the power of words," said Molly. "For, you see, I am...an *actress!*"

She pulled her paw down in front of her face to do a slight (yet extremely dramatic) head bow.

"She will, indubitably, shred the dogg to pieces," added her father, who was hovering over her shoulder.

"Well, we're looking forward to seeing you in action, Molly," said the ferret. "We hope you tear into that dogg the way a jackal tears into roadkill. But, wait. Here comes your opponent. Ladies and gentlemen, here he is, scampering up the red carpet, tail wagging, tongue lolling, ears perked up. It's the Dogg Scout himself. Here comes Molly's opponent, Oscar!"

Molly turned slightly as the cameras swung sideways to record Oscar's entrance.

She saw Oscar with his goofy tongue lolling out of his mouth. His happy tail wagging. His floppy paws bouncing up and down as he bounded up the red carpet.

And the strangest thing happened.

Molly almost couldn't breathe. Her heart was racing. Her white cheeks went slightly pink.

She was overcome with joy.

She was so happy to see him again.

"Oscar," Molly gasped under her smile.

She moved to give him a big hug.

But the television producer and her parents and even one of the security baboons grabbed her from behind.

"What do you think you're doing, Molly?" hissed her father.

"I want to hug Oscar. We went through so much together. And he looks all healed and—"

"You want to *hug* him?" said the ferret, as if

she couldn't believe her own ears. "Where is the drama in that, Molly? Your fans did not come here tonight to see a hug-fest. They came for a slug-fest! They want conflict, Molly. Action. Theater. Spectacle. And a good actress always gives her audience what they came to see!"

"Listen to the ferret, dear," said Molly's mother. "And remember: You're a katt! That boy is a dirty, disgusting—not to mention dumb—dogg!"

"Yes, mother," said Molly, dropping her eyes and shoulders.

"Come along," said her father, as he took Molly by the elbow and ushered her into the auditorium. "We should go inside, immediately!"

Molly did what her father told her to do.

After all, she always did what her daddy told her to do. She was a good katt.

Chapter 59

Oscar couldn't believe all the bright lights blinding him when he stepped up to his podium in front of the television cameras.

Molly was on the other side of the stage, standing behind her podium, looking like a glamorous movie star.

Somebody said they would be on the air, live, in five, four, three, two...

The audience clapped, cheered, and went crazy (maybe because there was a big blinking sign telling them to CLAP, CHEER, AND GO CRAZY).

Somewhere, a band struck up a dramatic theme song. Lights swung across the stage. Cameras swooped around on booms and cranes. The whole thing reminded Oscar of one of his favorite reality TV shows: *Doggs Got Talent*.

"Good evening, everybody," said the ferret at center stage. "Welcome to a special, *live* presentation of *Sworn Enemies for Life*! First up—the lightning round!"

Thunder clapped. Strobe lights flashed. Oscar wanted to go hide under his bed. He was afraid of lightning and thunder.

"Okay, Molly and Oscar. Here come a series of rapid-fire questions," said the ferret. "Molly, you go first. When I think about doggs I think about... fill in the blank!"

"Their smelly farts," said Molly, smoothly.

The audience roared with laughter and applause.

"Oscar? Your turn. Katts remind me of my worst...fill in the blank."

"Um, my worst...my worst..."

"I already said that part," joked the ferret. "You need to fill in what comes after that."

"Okay. Sure."

Oscar would've been sweating profusely except doggs don't sweat, they just pant. So he did that.

"Um, does it have to be something bad?" he asked while panting heavily.

"Uh, yeah."

"Because, all of a sudden, I was thinking about liverwurst."

"Excuse me?"

"It's a kind of meat," Oscar mumbled. "I like meat. And you said 'worst' which reminded me of liverwurst. I love the stuff. It's soft and meaty and…"

"Moving on," said the ferret. "Molly. Through what part of their body do doggs sweat?"

Molly shrugged. "I don't know. Their butts?"

More laughter. A buzzer scronked.

"Sorry. The correct answer is 'their mouths.'"

"Ewww. That's gross."

"I know. Okay, Oscar. What is the scientific name for fear of katts?"

"Oh, um, I think that's ailurophobia. I looked it up once because I was wondering why my whole family seemed to be so afraid of—"

"One-word answers will do, Oscar."

"I'm sorry."

"You sure are!" shouted one of the katts in the audience. All the other katts laughed.

Several doggs barked and growled.

The moderator led Oscar and Molly through a half dozen more quick questions. Molly was brilliant. Oscar was a mess.

"Let's move on to the main event," said the ferret, just when Oscar thought the torture would never end. "We want the inside scoop. What happened out there in the wilderness?"

"Ooooh," murmured the whole audience, leaning forward in their seats.

Everybody was interested in this.

Oscar was so nervous his mouth was drier than a rawhide chew that's been sitting in the sun for six months. He really, really wished there was a toilet bowl he could go drink out of.

Then things got even worse.

"Oscar?" said the ferret. "You go first."

Chapter 60

Um, okay," said Oscar. "My family and I were on our way to the Western Frontier Park when Dad got in this road rage race with a snooty katt family..."

"We won!" his dad shouted from the audience.

"Anyhoo," said Oscar, his tail sagging between his legs. "After some fun days at the dogg camp, I went chasing after a flying squirrel and got lost."

"Typical dogg!" sniffed the ferret. The katts in the crowd chuckled.

"I got lost because I chased a butterfly," said Molly.

"Awwwww," sighed all the katts. "A butterfly. How sweeeeet."

"You mean stupid!" snarled the doggs.

"That night I was walking around in circles, trying to find my way back to camp," said Oscar, "and I came across a wild mountain lion."

The whole crowd gasped in horror.

"Later," said Oscar, "I met Molly. Someone had nipped her ear and tail."

"You!" screamed the katts. "Ear nipper! Tail biter!"

"No. I didn't do it. I promise."

"Tell them, Molly. Tell them it was the mountain lion and the fox, not me."

Molly looked out into the audience. To where her family was sitting. They were hissing and swatting at Oscar's family across the aisle. And then...

Silence. She didn't say a word.

Oscar's ears and tail sank. Had he imagined all those nice, warm moments with Molly? How could she be so different from that lost katt in the woods?

"Well, Oscar," joked the moderator, "it sounds like you're the only one *lyin'* here! Molly? You tell us. What happened next?"

Molly was quiet. She was watching Oscar, the expression on her face unreadable.

"Molly?" the ferret pressed.

"Well, um, okay." Now Molly sounded nervous. And, from the look on her face, she was feeling kind of queasy. Oscar wondered if she'd had nacho-flavored dogg food for dinner, too.

"The, uh, dogg, he chased me..."

All the katts hissed.

"He also accused me of stealing all his food."

"I did," said Oscar. "And that was wrong. But I was very hungry so I wasn't thinking clearly. Turns out the mountain lion stole my food and shredded my knapsack. Molly's claws are too dainty to rip up fabric like that."

"It's true," said Molly, showing everybody her manicure.

The katts in the crowd purred.

"We ate bark and stuff," said Oscar. "One time, Molly found us berries. We shared them."

"Liar! You probably stole them from her!" a katt shouted.

Oscar started to whimper. He was telling the truth but everyone was yelling at him. All he wanted was to lie in his dogg bed under a blanket.

And never see Molly again for as long as he lived.

Then Molly's voice rang out. "I want all the katts to hear this," she said. "After being on my own for so long, I realized something."

"That you were trapped in the wilderness with your sworn enemy?" asked the ferret, her eyes wide.

"No." This time, Molly didn't look out into the audience for her family. She looked right at Oscar! "I realized that Oscar and I would have a better chance of surviving if we..." she paused and smiled at Oscar. "...called a truce."

"*What?*" screeched the ferret.

"Boo!" shouted the katts.

"Never!" shouted the doggs. "*No truce! No truce!*"

The hungry cameras rolled in for tighter shots.

Chapter 61

Oooh," said the ferret, greedily rubbing her paws together. "This is getting juicy! You called a truce and Oscar immediately broke it, right?"

"No," said Molly. "We helped each other. In fact, one time, we were on a cliff. Remember, Oscar?"

Oscar nodded. "And a weaselboar lowered its tusks and came charging right at us!"

"Oscar shielded me. Took a tusk to his chest and got that big gash."

"But Molly knew all about herbs and medicines. She helped heal me."

"It was the least I could do," Molly said modestly. "I would've lost one of my nine lives to that weaselboar if it weren't for him. Thank you, Oscar."

"Boo!" shouted the crowd. "Get those kids off the stage! He's a disgrace to doggs! She's a kattastrophe!"

A clump of doggs started hooting and howling at the moon, even though they were indoors. Several alley katts took to caterwauling and yelping. All the other creatures were grunting and groaning and ooh-ooh-ooh-ing in disapproval.

This show wasn't turning out as advertised.

"Let's get back on topic!" yelled the ferret. She had to shout to be heard over the uproar of several thousand angry creatures stuffed into an oversold auditorium. "Tell us why you hate Oscar, Molly."

"I don't hate him at all," she said proudly. "Oscar ferried me across a stream. He saved me from a marauding eagle even though he was badly hurt. I couldn't have asked for a better animal to be lost with."

"No, no, no!" cried the crowd, stomping their paws and hooves on the floor. "Booooooo!"

Finally, Oscar had had enough.

"Why don't you all just sit down and shut up!" he barked.

"We're trying to tell you that we saved each other's lives!" said Molly.

"We helped each other," said Oscar. "Then some other creatures helped us, too!"

"It's what they do in the wilderness!" said Molly. "They work together."

"And that's what we did the whole time we were together. And Molly was amazing out there! She's so smart it's scary."

"And Oscar's incredible! You should see him run, folks. Not just sprints. This dogg can go the distance! He's my hero!"

And then Molly did something even more amazing.

She leapt across the stage, grabbed Oscar, and kissed him!

Oscar thought he might faint.

"Did not see that coming," he muttered.

The audience was stunned.

They stopped booing and growling and yowling.

They stood there speechless. Their mouths hanging open. Their eyes wide.

They could not believe what they had just seen.

The ferret looked shocked.

There was no noise at all in the auditorium.

Except, finally, faintly—the sound of two creatures clapping.

They were Molly and Oscar's mothers!

Then, like a wave, the applause started to ripple across the room. At first it was cautious and unsure.

But then it grew louder.

And louder.

And louder still!

Even Oscar and Molly's fathers were clapping. And crying.

(Oscar's dad would later say that his eyes were watery because he's allergic to katts.)

Before long, everybody in the auditorium was cheering for Oscar and Molly and this strange idea of different creatures helping each other.

Oscar was so happy, his right rear leg started kicking.

Molly just purred.

Chapter 62

While the crowd cheered and clapped, Molly leaned in and whispered into Oscar's ear.

"That kiss was a little bit of theater," she told him. "You know—make believe. I was just pretending."

"Oh," said Oscar. He tried to lift his sagging tail but it seemed so heavy.

"Hey, I told you—I'm an excellent actress. That's what the scene needed. A kiss to shock the audience. An actress always gives the scene what it needs to move forward."

Oscar nodded. He wasn't going to let Molly see how much she'd just hurt his feelings. Because he was a dogg. Doggs weren't supposed to have sad feelings. At least, not for very long.

"Yeah, I knew you were faking it, Molly...I mean Miss Hissleton. I really shouldn't call you by your first name, right? We're not friends. Never have been, never will be. I mean, how could we be friends? You're a katt. I'm a dogg. I get it."

Molly grinned. "Well, actually you don't get it, goofball."

"Huh?"

"I was acting just now."

"Huh?"

"We *are* friends. In fact, after everything we went through together, I'd say we're the best of friends. BFFs, even. Best Friends Forever. I guess that's what happens when you save each other's lives on a daily basis. I'm sorry it took me awhile to understand how much you mean to me. I'll never forget it from now on."

Oscar was so happy, his tail nearly thumped

a hole in the stage floor. He grabbed Molly's paw and held it high.

It brought the house down.

Chapter 63

The next summer, two enraged drivers were racing their cars toward the Western Frontier Park.

One was full of katts. The other carried doggs.

"Aw, cheese on a biscuit!" growled the dogg behind the wheel of the car on the left. "That crazy katt up there hocked up a hairball and splattered it all over my windshield!"

He floored his accelerator. The car sped up.

"Brody?" said his wife, holding on to an overhead handle for dear life. "Did you forget to take your distemper shot this morning?"

"No, Trixie. But I am gonna run that katt off the road."

"You're scaring me!"

"Then sit on a wee-wee pad!"

The dogg car pulled alongside the katt car.

"Hey, fish breath!" shouted the dogg.

"Doggs," sneered the katt driver. "The more they bark, the less I care."

"You want some of this?" asked the dogg, balling up his paw.

"Some of what? Your ignorance or your stupidity?"

When they were maybe one hundred yards away from the entrance to the Western Frontier Park, the two drivers heard a siren. They both looked up at their rearview mirrors and saw...

A katt wearing a helmet with a twirling red light riding on the back of a very fast running dogg.

"Pull over, please!" called the katt through a bullhorn. Her diction was extremely good. Her delivery, very dramatic.

The two drivers did as they were told, even

303

though the katt and dogg law enforcement offi-
cers appeared to be very young.

The athletic dogg sprang up and over the two
parked vehicles and spun around so his katt passenger could address the two drivers.

"My name is Park Ranger Molly. This is my
partner, Park Ranger Oscar."

Oscar wagged his tail and panted.

"You are about to enter the Western Frontier
Park, folks," said Molly sternly. Stern was one of
her best emotions.

"You're leaving so-called civilization," said
Oscar. "So, new rules."

"Hey," said the driver of the dogg vehicle. "I've
seen you two kids on TV."

Molly smiled. It was fun being famous.

Oscar grinned, too. It was fun spending the
summer with his best pal. Especially since they
got to be in charge of stuff like welcoming new
guests.

"Now then," said Oscar, "if you will kindly
proceed to the brand new Katt and Dogg Campground."

"Huh?" said the dogg driver.

"The Katt and Dogg Campground," said Molly proudly. "Out here, katts and doggs dwell together in peace and harmony."

"Or they will go home," said Oscar. "That work for you?"

The dogg driver looked to his wife and the eager puppies in the backseat.

"Sure," he said. "We'll give it a try."

"As will we," said the katt driver with a sigh.

Oscar's tail started wagging. "Who says you can't teach old doggs new tricks?"

"Old katts, too!" said Molly.

Molly and Oscar laughed.

They did that a lot.

Because best friends forever always do.

PATTERSON FAMILY "KATTS AND DOGGS"

KATTS

- Red Boy
- Ebenezer ("Ebby")
- Inky
- Max ("Maximus Kittimus")
- Kismet
- Tippy-Tin
- Angel ("Angie Puddin'")
- Dukie
- Stubbs
- O'Mally
- Gizmo
- Black Bird
- GEO

DOGGS

- Lucky, Sheepdog
- Whiskey, Airedale Terrier
- Laddie ("Pickles"), Cairn Terrier
- Buddy, English Springer Spaniel
- Gypsy, Doberman Pinscher
- Mitzy, Dachshund

- Bumper, Shepherd
- Bingo, Manchester/Fox Terrier mix
- Deli, Labrador Retriever/Setter mix
- Bubba, Newfoundland
- Sparky ("Sparkle Plenty"), Corgi
- Nippy, Mutt
- Babe, German Shepherd
- Toffee, Irish Setter
- Madison, German Shepherd
- Chester, Labrador Retriever/Husky/Chow Chow mix
- Duffy, Labrador Retriever/English Setter mix
- Spotch, Labrador Retriever
- Finnegan, Mutt
- Stilch, Shetland Sheepdog mix
- Diablo, Labrador Retriever
- Beau ("Who Who Man"), Newfoundland/Labrador Retriever mix
- Moxie, Labrador Retriever
- Tazwasil, Jack Russell/Border Collie mix
- Sassy, English Labrador Retriever
- Shiraz, English Labrador Retriever
- Hallie, Labrador Retriever